A COLD DAY
FOR
MURDER

D1253614

DANA STABENOW

THE KATE SHUGAK SERIES

DANA STABENOW

A COLD DAY FOR MURDER

HEAD
ZEUS

An Aries Book

First published in the UK in 2013 by Head of Zeus Ltd
This edition published in 2023 by Head of Zeus,
part of Bloomsbury Publishing Plc

9 7 5 3 1 2 4 6 8

A CIP catalogue record for this book is available from
the British Library.

ISBN (paperback) 9781804549551
ISBN (ebook) 9781788548984

Printed and bound by CPI Group (UK) Ltd,
Croydon, CR0 4YY

Head of Zeus Ltd
5–8 Hardwick Street
London EC1R 4RG
WWW.HEADOFZEUS.COM

For Don Stabenow,
my very own personal air taxi service
and pyrotechnical adviser

CHAPTER 1

THEY CAME OUT OF the south late that morning on a black-and-silver Ski-doo LT. The driver had thick eyebrows and a thicker beard and a lush fur ruff around his hood, all rimmed with frost from the moisture of his breath. He was a big man, made larger by parka, down bib overalls, fur mukluks and thick fur gauntlets. His teeth were bared in a grin that was half-snarl. He looked like John Wayne ready to run the claim jumpers off his gold mine on that old White Mountain just a little southeast of Nome, if John Wayne had been outfitted by Eddie Bauer.

The man sitting behind him and clinging desperately to his seat was half his size and had no ruff around the edge of his hood. His face was a fragile layer of frost over skin drained a pasty white. He wore a down snowsuit at least three sizes too big for him, the bottoms of the legs coming down over his wingtip shoes. He wasn't smiling at all. He looked like Sam McGee from Tennessee before he was stuffed into the furnace of the *Alice May*.

The rending, tearing noise of the snow machine's engine echoed across the landscape and affronted the arctic peace of that December day. It startled a moose stripping the bark from a stand of spindly birches. It sent a beaver back into her den in a swift-running stream. It woke a bald eagle roosting in the top of a spruce, causing him to glare down on the two men with malevolent eyes. The sky was of that crystal clarity that comes only to lands of the far north in winter; light, translucent, wanting cloud and color. Only the first blush of sunrise outlined the jagged peaks of mountains to the east, though it was well past nine in the morning. The snow was layered in graceful white curves beneath the alder and spruce and cottonwood, all the trees except for the spruce spare and leafless, though even the green spines of the spruce seemed faded to black this morning.

"I gotta take a leak," the man in back yelled in the driver's ear.

"You don't want to step off into the snow anywhere near here," the driver roared over the noise of the machine.

"Why not?" the passenger yelled back. A thin shard of ice cracked and slid from his cheek.

"It's deeper than it looks, probably over your head. You could founder here and never come up for air. Just hang on. It's not far now."

The machine lurched and skidded around a clump of trees, and the passenger held on and muttered to himself through clenched teeth. The big man's grin broadened.

Without warning they burst into a clearing. The big man reduced speed so abruptly that his passenger was thrown forward. When he hauled himself upright again and looked around, his first impression of the winter scene laid out before him was that it was just too immaculate, too orderly, too perfect to exist in a world of flawed, disorderly and imperfect men.

The log cabin in the clearing sat on the edge of a bluff that fell a hundred feet to the half-frozen Kanuyaq River below. Beyond the far bank of the river the land rose swiftly into the sharp peaks of the Quilak Mountains. The cabin, looking more as if it had grown there naturally rather than been built by human hands, stood at the center of a small semicircle of buildings. At the left and slightly to the back there was an outhouse, tall, spare and functional. Several depressions in the snow around it indicated it had been moved more than once, which gave the man on the snow machine some idea of how long the homestead had been there. Next was a combined garage and shop, through the open door of which could be seen a snow machine, a small truck and assorted related gear. He found the sight of these indubitably twentieth-century products infinitely reassuring. Next to the cabin stood an elevated stand for a dozen fifty-five-gallon barrels of Chevron diesel fuel, stacked on their sides. Immediately to the right of the cabin was a greenhouse, its Visqueen panels opaque with frost. Next to it and completing the semicircle stood a cache elevated some ten feet in the air on peeled log stilts, with a narrow ladder leading to its single door.

Paths through the drifts of snow had been cut with almost surgical precision, linking every structure to its neighbor. The resulting half-circle was packed firm between tidy berms as level as a clipped hedge. One trail led directly to the wood pile, which the man judged held at least three cords, split as neatly as they were stacked. Another pile of unsplit rounds stood next to the chopping block.

There were no footprints outside the trails. It seemed that this was one homesteader who kept herself to herself.

The glow of the wood of each structure testified to a yearly application of log oil. There wasn't a shake missing from any of the roofs. The usual dump of tires too worn to use but too good to throw away, the pile of leftover lumber cut in odd lengths but still good for something, someday, the stack of Blazo boxes to be used for shelves, the shiny hill of Blazo tins someday to carry water, the haphazard mound of empty, rusting fifty-five-gallon drums to be cut into stoves when the old one wore out, all these staples were missing. It was most unbushlike and positively unAlaskan. He had a suspicion that when the snow melted the grass wouldn't dare to grow more than an inch tall, or the tomatoes in the greenhouse bear less than twelve to the vine. He was assailed by an unexpected and entirely unaccustomed feeling of inadequacy, and wished suddenly that he had taken the time to search out a parka and boots, the winter uniform of the Alaskan bush, before making this pilgrimage. At least then he would have been properly dressed to meet Jack London, who was undoubtedly inside the cabin in front of him, writing "To Build a Fire" and making countless future generations of Alaskan junior high English students miserable in the process. He would have been unsurprised to see Samuel Benton Steele mushing up the trail in his red Mountie coat and flat-brimmed Mountie hat. He would merely have turned to look for Soapy Smith moving fast in the other direction. He realized finally that his mouth was hanging half-open, closed it with something of a snap and wondered what kind of time warp they had wandered through on the way here, and if they would be able to find it again on the return to their own century.

The big man switched off the engine. The waiting silence fell like a vengeful blow and his passenger was temporarily stunned by it. He rallied. "All this scene needs is the Northern Lights," he said, "and we could paint it on a gold pan and get twenty bucks for it off the little old lady from Duluth."

The big man grinned a little.

The smaller man took a deep breath and the frozen air burned into his lungs. Unused to it, he coughed. "So this is her place?"

"This is it," the big man confirmed, his deep voice rumbling over the clearing. As if to confirm his words, they heard the door to the cabin slam shut. The other man raised his eyebrows, cracking more ice off his face.

"Well, at least now we know she's home," the big man said placidly, and dismounted.

"Son of a bitch, what is that?" his passenger said, his face if possible becoming even more colorless.

The big man looked up to see an enormous gray animal with a stiff ruff and a plumed tail trotting across the yard in their direction, silent and purposeful. "Dog," he said laconically.

"Dog, huh?" the other man said, trying and failing to look away from the animal's unflinching yellow eyes. He groped in his pocket until his gloved fingers wrapped around the comforting butt of his .38 Police Special. He looked up to find those yellow eyes fixed on him with a thoughtful, considering expression, and he froze. "Looks like a goddam wolf to me," he said finally, trying hard to match the other man's nonchalance.

"Nah," the big man said, holding out one hand, fingers curled, palm down. "Only half. Hey, Mutt, how are you, girl?" She extended a cautious nose, sniffed twice and sneezed. Her tail gave a perfunctory wag. She looked from the first man to the second and seemed to raise one eyebrow. "Hold out your hand," the big man said.

"What?"

"Make a fist, palm down, hold it out."

The other man swallowed, mentally bid his hand goodbye and obeyed. Mutt sniffed it, looked him over a third time in a way that made him hope he wasn't breathing in an aggressive manner, and then stood to one side, clearly waiting to escort them to the door of the cabin.

"There's the outhouse," the big man said, pointing.

"What?"

"You said you wanted to take a leak."

He looked from dog to outhouse and back to the dog. "Not that bad."

"That's some fucking doorman you've got out there," he said, once he was safely inside the cabin and the door securely latched behind him.

"Can I offer you a drink?" Her voice was odd, too loud for a whisper, not low enough for a growl, and painfully rough, like a dull saw ripping through old cement.

"I'll take whatever you got, whiskey, vodka, the first bottle you grab." The passenger had stripped off his outsize snowsuit to reveal a pin-striped three-piece suit complete with knotted tie and gold watch attached to a chain that stretched over a small, round potbelly the suit had been fighting ever since his teens.

She paused momentarily, taking in this sartorial splendor with a long, speculative survey that reminded him uncomfortably of the dog outside. "Coffee?" she said. "Or I could mix up some lemonade."

"Coffee's fine, Kate," the big man said. The suit felt like crying.

"It's on the stove." She jerked her chin. "Mugs and spoons and sugar on the shelf to the left."

The big man smiled down at her. "I know where the mugs are."

She didn't smile back.

The mugs were utilitarian white porcelain and the coffee was nectar and ambrosia. By his second cup the suit had defrosted enough to revert to type, to examine and inventory the scene.

The interior of the cabin was as neat as its exterior, maybe neater, neat enough to make his teeth ache. It reminded him of the cabin of a sailboat with one of those persnickety old bachelor skippers; there was by God a place for everything and everything had by God better be in its place. Kerosene lamps hissed gently from every corner of the room, making the cabin, unlike so many of its shadowy, smoky little contemporaries in the Alaskan bush, well lit. The plank walls, too, were sanded and finished. The first floor, some twenty-five feet square, was a living room, dining room and kitchen combined; a ladder led to a loft that presumably served as a bedroom, tucked away beneath the rear half of the roof's steep pitch. He estimated eleven hundred square feet of living space altogether, and was disposed to approve of the way it was arranged.

An oil stove for cooking took up the center of the left wall, facing a wood stove on the right wall, both of them going. A tall blue enamel coffeepot stood on the oil stove. A steaming, gallon-size teakettle sat on the wood stove's large surface, and a large round tin tub hung on the wall behind it. A counter, interrupted by a large, shallow sink with a pump handle, ran from the door to the oil stove, shelves above and below filled with orderly stacks of dishes, pots and pans and foodstuffs. A small square dining table covered with a faded red-and-white checked oilskin stood in the rear left-hand corner next to the oil stove. There were two upright wooden chairs, old but sturdy. On a shelf above were half a dozen decks of cards, poker chips and a Scrabble game. A wide, built-in bench ran along the back wall and around the rear right-hand corner, padded with foam rubber and upholstered in a deep blue canvas fabric. Over the bench built-in shelves bore a battery-operated cassette player and tidy stacks of cassette tapes. He read some of the artists' names out loud. "Peter, Paul and Mary, John Fogerty, Jimmy Buffet," he said, and turned with a friendly smile. "All your major American philosophers. We'll get along, Ms. Shugak."

She looked perfectly calm, her lips unsmiling, but there was a feeling of something barely leashed in her brown eyes when she paused in her bread making to look him over, head to toe, in a glance that once again took in his polished loafers, his immaculate suit and his crisply knotted tie. He checked an impulse to see if his fly was zipped. "I wasn't aware we had to," she said without inflection, and turned back to the counter.

The suit turned to the big man, whose expression, if possible, was even harder to read than the woman's. The suit shrugged and continued his inspection. Between the wood stove and the door were bookshelves, reaching around the corner of the house and from floor to ceiling, every one of them crammed with books. Curious, he ran his finger down their spines, and found *New Hampshire* wedged in between *Pale Gray for Guilt* and *Citizen of the Galaxy*. He cast a glance at the woman's unresponsive back, and opened the slim volume. Many of the pages were dog-eared, with notes penciled in the margins in a small, neat, entirely illegible hand. He closed the book and then allowed it to fall open where it would, and read part of a poem about a man who burned down his house for the fire insurance so he could buy a telescope. There were no notes on that page, only the smooth feeling on his fingertips of words on paper worn thin with reading. He replaced the book and strummed the strings of the dusty guitar hanging next to the shelving. It was out of tune. It had been out of tune for a long time.

"Hey." The woman was looking over at him, her eyes hard. "Do you mind?"

8

He dropped his hand. The silence in the little cabin bothered him. He had never been greeted with anything less than outright rejoicing in the Alaskan bush during the winter, or during the summer, either, any summer you could find anyone home. Especially at isolated homesteads like this one.

He swung around and took his first real look at the woman who wasn't even curious enough to ask his name. The woman who, until fourteen months ago, had been the acknowledged star of the Anchorage District Attorney's investigative staff. Who had the highest conviction rate in the state's history for that position. Whose very presence on the prosecution's witness list had induced defense lawyers to throw in their briefs and plea-bargain. Who had successfully resisted three determined efforts on the part of the FBI to recruit her.

Twenty-nine or thirty, he judged, which if she had had a year of training after college before going to work for Morgan would be about right. Five feet tall, no more, maybe a hundred and ten pounds. She had the burnished bronze skin and high, flat cheekbones of her race, with curiously light brown eyes tilted up at her temples, all of it framed by a shining fall of utterly black, utterly straight hair. The fabric of her red plaid shirt strained across her square shoulders and the swell of her breasts, and her Levis were worn white at butt and knees. She moved like a cat, all controlled muscle and natural grace, wary but assured. He wondered idly if she would be like a cat in bed, and then he remembered his wife and the last narrowly averted action for divorce and reined in his imagination. From the vibrations he was picking up between her and the big man he would never have a chance to test his luck, anyway.

Then she bent down to bring another scoop of flour up from the sack on the floor, and he sucked in his breath. For a moment her collar had fallen away and he had seen the scar, twisted and ugly and still angry in color. It crossed her throat almost from ear to ear. That explains the voice, he thought, shaken. Why hadn't she gone to a plastic surgeon and had that fixed, or at least had the scar tissue trimmed and reduced in size? He looked up to see the big man watching him out of blue eyes that held a clear warning. His own gaze faltered and fell.

But she had noticed his reaction. Her eyes narrowed. She lifted one hand as if to button her shirt up to the collar, hesitated, and let it fall. "What do you want, Jack?" she said abruptly.

The big man lowered his six-foot-two, two-hundred-and-twenty-pound frame down on the homemade couch, which groaned in protest, sipped at his coffee and wiped the moisture from his thick black mustache. He had hung his parka without looking for the hook, found the sugar on the right shelf the first time and settled himself on the softest spot on the couch without missing a beat. He looked relaxed, even at home, the suit thought. The woman evidently thought so, too, and her generous mouth tightened into a thin line.

"Parks Department's lost a ranger," the big man said.

She floured the counter and turned the dough out of the pan.

The big man's imperturbable voice went on. "He's been missing about six weeks."

She kneaded flour into the dough and folded it over once, twice, again. "He couldn't have lost himself in a snowstorm and froze to death like most of them do?"

"He could have, but we don't think so."

"Who's we?"

"This is Fred Gamble, FBI."

She looked the suit over and lifted one corner of her mouth in a faint smile that could not in any way be construed as friendly. "The FBI? Well, well, well."

"He came to us for help, since it's our jurisdiction. More or less. So as a professional courtesy I sent in an investigator from our office."

The woman's flour-covered hands were still for a moment, as she raised her eyes to glance briefly out the window over the sink. Gamble thought she was going to speak, but she resumed her task without comment.

The big man looked into his coffee mug as if it held the answers to the mysteries of the universe. "I haven't heard from him in two weeks. Since he called in from Niniltna the day after he arrived."

She folded another cup of flour into the dough and said, "What's the FBI doing looking for a lost park ranger?" She paused, and said slowly, "What's so special about this particular ranger?"

The big man gave her unresponsive back a slight, approving smile. "His father."

"Who is?"

"A congressman from Ohio."

She gave a short, unamused laugh and shook her head, giving the suit a sardonic glance. "Oh ho ho."

"Yeah."

Gamble tugged at his tie, which felt a bit tight.

"So you sent in an investigator," she said.

"Yes."

"When? Exactly."

"Two weeks and two days ago, exactly."

"And now he's missing, too."

"Yes."

"And you don't think both of them could have stumbled into a snowdrift."

"No. Not when the investigator went in specifically to look for the ranger."

"Maybe it was the same snowdrift."

"No."

"No." She worked the dough, her shoulders stiff and angry. "And now you want me to go in."

"The feds want the best. I recommended you. I told them you know the Park better than anyone. You were born here, raised here. Hell, you're related to half the people in it."

She sent him a black, unfriendly look, which he met without flinching. "Why should I help you?"

He shrugged and drained his cup, and stood to refill it. "You've been pouting up here for over a year. From what I read outside just now you haven't left the homestead since the first snow." He met her eyes with a bland expression. "What's next? You going to give the spruce trees a manicure?"

Her thick, straight brows met in a single line across her forehead. "Maybe I just like living alone," she snapped. "And maybe you should get out of here so I can get on with it."

"And maybe," he said, "you could use a little excitement right about now. At least looking for a couple of missing persons would give you the chance to talk to someone. Taken a vow of silence, Kate?" In spite of his outward appearance of calm, the big man's tone was barbed.

Her hands stilled and she fixed him with a stony gaze. "Dream on, Jack. I've got my books and my music, so I'm not bored. I run a couple traps, I pan a little gold, I bag a few tourists in season and raft them down the Kanuyaq, so I'm not broke. I guided a couple of hunting parties this fall and took my fee in meat, so the cache is full. I won't starve." The corners of her mouth curled, and she added, her words a deliberate taunt, "And Ken comes up from town every few weeks. So I'm not even horny."

The big man's jaw set hard, but he met her eyes without flinching. Gamble shifted in his seat and wished he'd never insisted on coming with Morgan to this godforsaken place, living legend or no. He cleared his throat gently. "Listen, folks," he said, examining his finger-nails, "I get the feeling that if I weren't here the two of you would either duke it out or hit the sack or maybe both, and maybe that would be a good thing, but at this moment I don't really give a flying fuck about you or your personal problems. All I want is to get the Honorable Marcus A. Miller, representative of the great state of Ohio, off my goddam back. Now, what do you say?"

The flush in her cheeks could have been from the heat of the stove. She held the big man's gaze for another long moment, and then whipped around and kneaded vigorously. "There's nothing you have I need or want, Jack, so don't ask me for any favors. You won't be able to pay them back."

The fire crackled in the wood stove. Kate divided the dough into loaves and opened the oven on the oil stove to check the temperature. Gamble got up and refilled his coffee cup for the third time. The big man stirred, and said into the silence, "You busted that bootlegger for the Niniltna Corporation."

There was a brief pause. "That was different."

"Kate—"

"Shut up about that, Jack. Just—shut up about it. Okay?"

Into the following silence Gamble said gently, "We'll pay you."

She shrugged.

"Four hundred a day and expenses."

She didn't even bother to shrug this time.

The big man finished his coffee and motioned for the other man to do the same. He set both cups in the sink, standing next to her without looking at her. He worked the pump and rinsed them out and placed them upside down in the drainer. He dried his hands and pulled down his parka. Before shrugging into it, he reached into a deep pocket and pulled out a manila folder, which he tossed on the table. On his way out he paused at the door, glanced over his shoulder at Kate, up to her elbows in bread dough, and smiled to himself.

The woman's voice came out low and husky. "Jack."

He paused on the doorstep.

"Which investigator did you send in?" It was a question, but she didn't sound curious. She sounded as if she already knew.

He lifted the latch and opened the door. "Dahl went in." He paused, and added gently, "He had the most bush experience, you see. All that personal, one-on-one training you gave him." He stepped outside and said over his shoulder, "I left the ranger's file on the table. Get Bobby to call me when you have something."

• • •

Outside, Gamble looked at him and said, "Where'd she get that scar?" Jack busied himself with the starter on the engine, and Gamble repeated, "Morgan. Where did she get that scar?"

The other man sighed, and said flatly, "In a knife fight with a child molester."

Gamble stared at him. "Jesus Christ. That part of the story is true, then?"

"Yeah." The big man's eyes were bleak.

"Jesus Christ," Gamble repeated. "What happened?"

Jack unscrewed the gas cap and rocked the snow machine back and forth, peering inside the tank. "Somebody made an anonymous call to Family Services, reporting a father of five to be a habitual abuser of all five children. They called us. Kate went to check it out and caught him in the act with the four-year-old."

Gamble closed his eyes and shook his head. "You nail the perp?"

Morgan unhooked the jerry can from the back of the machine and emptied it into the gas tank. "He's dead."

Gamble's sigh was long and drawn out. "Uh-huh." He stared at the cabin. The sun was out by now, but he felt cold all the way through. "When did this happen?"

"Fourteen months, thirteen days." The big man thought for a moment, and added, "And seven hours ago."

Gamble stared at him. "You're sure about the time frame?"

The big man's ruddy cheeks darkened a little. It could have been the cold. He didn't answer.

Gamble thought for a moment. "That would have been about the time she left the D.A.'s office."

"About."

"Disability?"

"Nope. Quit." Morgan replaced the gas cap and gave it a final twist. He raised his eyes to stare at the closed cabin door, before which Mutt sat, alert, motionless, looking at them with her ears up and her yellow eyes unblinking. "She walked out of the hospital the next day and tacked a letter of resignation to my door with the knife she took off the perp."

"Jesus Christ," Gamble said for the third time.

"Yeah," Jack said. "Hell of a mess. His blood was still all

15

over the blade." He shook his head disapprovingly. "Lousy crime scene inventory. APD should never have let her leave with it." The big man looked steadily at the cabin, as if by sheer will his gaze would penetrate the walls and seek out the woman inside. "She used to sing."

Gamble maintained a hopeful silence. It was the first remark Morgan had made all day that Gamble hadn't had to drag out of him.

"She knows all the words to every high sea chantey ever written down," Morgan said softly.

Gamble waited, but Morgan said nothing more. He started the engine and they climbed on the snow machine. Over the noise of the engine Gamble shouted, "Well?"

Morgan looked back at the cabin. "She'll do it."

Gamble snorted.

"She'll do it," the big man repeated. "Roll those snowsuit legs down or your feet'll get frostbite. And next time for chrissake bring some goddam boots." He pushed off with one foot and the machine began to slide forward.

"It's your call, Jack, but are you sure we shouldn't find someone else to do this job?" Gamble persisted. "You sure she'll look for them?"

"I'm sure," the big man said. His certainty did not sound as if it gave him any joy.

• • •

Jerking awake at three the next morning, fleeing dark dreams of an endless procession of frightened, bleeding children begging her not to hurt their parents, Kate, sweating, trembling, swearing loudly to drown out the blood pounding in her ears, came to the same conclusion. The hauntings would continue no matter what she did; she knew that already. But for a time, perhaps, the ghosts would take on a different shape, mouth different words, stare accusingly for different reasons. It was enough.

CHAPTER 2

THE PARK OCCUPIED TWENTY million acres, almost four times the size of Denali National Park but with less than one percent of the tourists. It was bordered on the north and east by the Quilak Mountains, a coastal range that wandered back and forth over the Alaska-Canada border and whose tallest peaks shared an average height of sixteen thousand feet, not the twenty thousand feet of Denali's McKinley, but high enough to awe and to challenge. Glaciers three thousand feet thick and thirty miles long poked their cold tongues out of every pass, all of them in recession, but only slowly and very, very reluctantly. On the south was the Gulf of Alaska; in the west the more or less parallel lines of the TransAlaska Pipeline, the pipeline haul road and the single north-south track of the Alaska Railroad. The land, gently sloping and open in the west, rose rapidly into the mountains in the east and was drained by the Kanuyaq River. Two hundred and fifty miles long including every twist and turn, the river was frozen over in winter, swollen with glacial runoff and salmon in summer, wide, shallow and navigable for less than six months out of the year. The Park's coast was almost impenetrable from the sea, choked with coastal rain forest made of Sitka spruce, hemlock, alder and devil's club. This thinned out as the land rose, until above the tree line there was nothing but kinnikinnick, rock and ice.

Hunters, among the Park's few tourists, came from the

South 48, Europe, Asia and Africa to hunt in the Park. Dall sheep roamed over the glaciers while caribou wandered from Alaska to Canada and back again. As the land was settled and cleared, more and more moose could be found up to their bellies in shallow lakes and streams, their mouths full of greens. There were even bison in the Park, transplanted there in 1950 and by 1980 numbering a hundred and thirty. There was one grizzly for every ten square miles; more than enough, everyone agreed. Gray wolf and wolverine, coyote and red fox, ground squirrels, lynx, beaver, land and sea otters, muskrat, mink, marmot, snowshoe hare and beaver made it a trapper's paradise. In every creek and tributary of the Kanuyaq that staple Alaskan food, the almighty salmon in all its species, ran and spawned and died, their offspring to travel deep into the Pacific, then return and begin the cycle once again.

The major difference between tourist mecca Denali National Park and this one was a road.

Denali had one.

The only road into the heart of this Park was the crumbling remnant of a railroad grade forty years old that had once supported the Kanuyaq River & Northern Railroad during its thirty-year exploitation of the richest copper deposit on the North American continent. It had been well engineered and well built, and in summer was flat and hard and drivable, if and when it received its monthly scraping by state road grader. After the first snow fell the state road crews stopped where the national park boundaries began.

But it was a wonderful park, rich in mountains, for it took in parts of the Mentasta, Nutzotin and Chugach ranges, as well as supporting the entire Quilak range. It boasted several hundred miles of coastline along Prince William Sound, site of one of the richest salmon fisheries in the world, and you could always fly in to fish, if you could fly, or could afford to pay someone who did. A shame that so few could, Park rats told each other, some even with straight faces.

There were dozens of airstrips within the Park, some sworn to by FAA charts, but between the time the chart was printed and the time the pilot with a ruptured oil line looked for them they would be overgrown by a hungry forest or eroded out of existence by a change of course in the Kanuyaq. There was a well-maintained 4,800-foot gravel strip at Niniltna, but tribal policemen met you on the runway and searched your plane for liquor and drugs, which, depending on what you were carrying in the back of your airplane, made putting down in Niniltna village something between a personal nuisance and a felony arrest.

And so, though it might in name be a park for all the people, in fact only those with access to a plane and the political muscle necessary to promote a permit were able to take advantage of all that pristine wilderness. With small plane rentals running $185 an hour wet and the customer paying the entire four-hour round-trip if the air taxi had no load going back, generally their only renters were park managers and United States senators and the occasional state governor, and their guests.

Yes, it was a great park, a spectacular park, a national treasure, everyone agreed, not least those who lived there. You just couldn't get at it.

● ● ●

There were eleven new loaves of bread, five wrapped in foil and stored outside in the cache. Kate put six in her backpack for Abel, since he was the only person she knew who could slay yeast with a single glare. She'd ruined the twelfth loaf when the pot holder slipped and she burned her fingers, and she'd thrown the loaf pan across the cabin in a fit of temper she was glad no one but Mutt was there to see.

Her temper lasted through the following morning. She stubbed her toe on the loft ladder. The handle of her brush broke off in mid-stroke in a tangle of hair. The wood stove's damper refused to cooperate when she went to stoke it for her absence, and it took a blasphemous half hour and a burn on her other hand to adjust it. She yanked on her snowsuit, stamped her feet into her shoepacs and wrenched the door to her cabin open, and Mutt took one look at her face and vanished.

"Thanks," Kate said, with awful civility. "I needed that." She slammed the door and a large icicle broke off the eaves of the cabin, narrowly missing her. She stalked out to the garage and checked the oil and gas on her Super Jag. The snow machine was Arctic Cat's top of the line, the compleat bush transportation, brand new last winter, with a track 156 inches long and 16 inches wide, a springer front end that made the going easier over deep snow, a 440-cc fan-cooled engine and a 108 Comet over-drive clutch. It averaged 120 miles to a tank of gas, had handlebar warmers and a storage box, and in spite of all the extras the dealer had drooled over in the showroom, after six weeks of idleness the engine didn't want to turn over so much as it wanted to lay down and die. Kate cursed, fluently and loudly. Mutt poked a cautious muzzle around the door and looked at her reproachfully. With an effort Kate restrained herself from hurling a crescent wrench at her beloved roommate.

"I can't wake up grumpy like ordinary people?" she demanded.

You never do, Mutt told her.

Kate sighed heavily and sat down on the snow machine. "You're right, Mutt," she said, holding out her hand. Mutt trotted over to stick her head under it. "But just because I've come to a decision and settled on a course of action doesn't mean I have to like it."

Of course not, Mutt said.

"I need somebody to blame," Kate said.

Anybody but me, Mutt said agreeably.

"How about Jack?"

Mutt looked doubtful, but the more Kate thought about it, the more likely and attractive a candidate Jack Morgan seemed. He had made it impossible for her to refuse to leave her warm and comfortable and private sanctuary, in the dead of winter, to get him out of a mess he himself had made, in a place she habitually avoided, teeming with too many people she had no wish to see. That she was working again for Jack poured salt in the wound. When she had seen him yesterday it had taken every ounce of self-control she had not to shame the very name of bush hospitality by refusing him so much as a cup of coffee.

"And I do too have someone to talk to," she said suddenly to Mutt. "I've got you. Vow of silence my ass."

Mutt licked her face with a large, wet and understanding tongue. Kate went back to work on the Jag.

The next time she pressed the starter the engine turned over, coughed twice and settled into a loud purr. She unhitched the sled and pushed the snow machine out of the shop. She checked the survival gear in its locker, took out the mosquito net that she had neglected to remove after the first frost and added a toothbrush and a change of underwear. She checked to see that the door to the cabin was unlocked. It was.

She couldn't think of anything else to delay her departure. She took a deep breath and squared her shoulders. "Ready, Mutt?"

Mutt was always ready to go anywhere. She leaped up behind Kate and with a roar of sound and a jerk they were off. It was another translucent arctic morning, the sky lightening imperceptibly toward the southeast but not yet prepared to commit to the full, grayish-pink flush of dawn.

• • •

Abel Int-Hout's homestead was three times the size of the one Kate had inherited from her father. It was located on an idyllic site at the head of a long, deep lake backed up against a Quilak foothill. Beginning where the lake left off, in six months there would be a wide, green strip of manicured grass, long enough to accommodate a twin-engine Beechcraft. Abel's current Cessna would be tied down close to the house, if that year it wasn't a Beaver on floats moored in the lake. This winter it was a Super Cub on skis, and the snow on the airstrip was solidly packed down with countless takeoffs and landings as Abel's friends from around the state flew in and out on visits.

Abel's house was no cabin. It had a screen door and windows, red-painted clapboard sides, a wide veranda running around three sides of the building, running hot and cold water and, most wonderful of all, an indoor flush toilet. The garden was modest as well, only an acre in size, covered in black plastic in summer, with neatly placed punctures through which Abel bullied the broccoli and the cauliflower into emerging. The greenhouse had more square feet than the house; there Abel grew tomatoes and pumpkins and one summer of glorious memory had even managed to produce some minuscule ears of sweet corn. The rows of peas and raspberries behind the greenhouse and the strawberry patch that threatened one day to overgrow the airstrip didn't seem hardly worth mentioning. A little way up the hill was a small cemetery, where two generations of Int-Houts lay at rest after long, productive lives of panning for gold, trapping beaver and marten and fishing for salmon and king crab. The most recent headstone was that of Abel's wife, Anna, dead three years.

Where Kate's cabin and outbuildings looked neat and well kept, Abel's looked like an advertisement for *Better Homesteads and Gardens*, and she never saw it without a sternly repressed pang of envy.

Abel didn't hold with snow machines so Kate left hers by the side of the rough-packed snow of the railroad bed and walked down the trail to the homestead. Mutt bounced along next to her, snapping at branches encased in delicate crystal shells and causing showers of the tinkling fragments to cascade down over them, looking up at Kate with an expression that just begged for play. Kate chased after her, and they were both out of breath when they reached the homestead. They were instantly surrounded by a large pack of dogs, most of them huskies or husky breeds, all trying to jump up on both of them at once and all barking a loud and vociferous welcome.

Mutt put up with it for about sixty seconds and then cut loose with a single sharp, shrill bark of her own. There was instantaneous silence. Half the pack flattened their ears and wagged conciliating tails, and the other half lay down, rolled over and waved their paws in the air. Mutt looked up at Kate with a smug expression.

"Yes, you are truly wonderful," Kate told her.

He'd heard them coming, and was waiting at the door. "What the hell you doing here?"

"Nice to see you, too, Abel."

He harrumphed loudly and gestured at her full arms. "What'd you bring me?"

"Six loaves of bread," she said, handing them over, "not that I should give you anything when I haven't had my moose roast."

"What the hell you going on about now, girl?"

She gestured at the long bundle encased in canvas, hanging from the bottom of his cache, the size of a haunch off a well-fed bull. "I thought I always got the first roast off the moose." He looked from the bundle to her and his leathery cheeks flushed. She said, laughing a little, "Better not let the fish hawks find you with that hanging there, Abel. They catch you hunting moose out of season, they'll take away your Cub and your Winchester and put you in jail for the rest of your life."

"Hell, girl," he said, giving her a tight grin, "you know I'm a subsistence hunter. Since they passed that law in 1980 I can shoot what I want, when I want in the Park, as long as I need it to eat."

She laughed again and held out her arms, and he snorted and came forward to give her a hug that bruised her ribs. "Come on in then, girl, if you're done making me out to be some kind of crook."

Abel Int-Hout looked like a fierce old eagle, his thinning white hair skinned back over his head, his proud beak of a nose jutting from between two faded but still very sharp blue eyes. Kate thought, not for the first time, that Abel Int-Hout stood on the front doorstep of his homestead the same way Tennyson's eagle clasped the crag with crooked hands, proud, possessive and fiercely protective of him and his.

He led the way into his kitchen. "What are you up to?" he said, pouring coffee into thick mugs. He set out a can of Carnation evaporated milk, a bowl of sugar, one spoon and a carton of Ding Dongs.

Kate drew a chair up to the table and rested her elbows on the oilskin tablecloth. "I'm on my way in to see emaaqa," she said.

His head came up and he looked at her out of his sharp old eyes. "You're going in to Niniltna?"

"Yes."

"Been a while since you've been home."

She said carefully, forgetting for a moment who she was speaking to, "Niniltna isn't home, Abel. It's only where I was born."

He snorted. "If you hate it all that much, why'd you pick the middle of the winter to mush in?"

"I'm not mushing."

He snorted again. "I heard. I swear, girl, I don't know why you bother with them infernal machines. They're dirty, noisy as hell, can't reproduce themselves, and they sure as shit ain't much company."

"No, Abel," she agreed in a meek voice, and refrained from pointing out that his Super Cub made more noise than half a dozen snow machines in full cry, and it couldn't reproduce itself, either. But then, it wasn't as if she loved the old man for his consistency.

Except for a flock of a dozen tame geese, seven cats and innumerable dogs, Abel lived quite alone on the homestead. He was a retired seiner whose children, disdaining the life of the backwoods, had all migrated to Cordova and Anchorage and Outside. Abel stayed where he was. It was his home. It was his life.

Abel had married into Kate's mother's family, and he was Kate's first cousin once removed or just her second cousin, they'd never decided which. Her father drowned in Prince William Sound when Kate was eight. Her mother had died two years before, and her grandmother had decreed that Kate would move to Niniltna and live with her. Eight-year-old Kate had stated flatly that she wouldn't go. Into this confrontation between irresistible force and immovable object stepped Abel. Abel took Kate into his home, letting her return to her father's homestead on weekends, making no other distinction between her and his own children unless it was that he liked her more than he did his own. They certainly had more in common.

Abel, lacking children with like interests, taught Kate everything her father was always going to but never quite had the time for. He taught her how to hunt the Sitka black-tailed deer by sitting still at the base of a tree, for hours if need be, to lull the deer into making the first move. How to mend gill nets so the sockeyes stayed put until they were picked, instead of ripping it to shreds so you had to go even deeper in debt to the cannery for new gear. How to gut a moose without slicing open the organs and making a green, smelly mess out of the process, and how to skin it, and how to cut it so that you got roasts and steaks instead of, as happened on her first two tries, a winter's supply of mooseburger.

She watched him pour the coffee, caught between affection and amusement. He looked up, his eyes glinting. "No comment? Not up to fighting with me today, is that it, girl?" Kate grinned without answering. "So why are you going to see Ekaterina?"

She drank coffee. "I'm looking for somebody."

"Who?"

"Two somebodies, actually, a park ranger named Mark

27

Miller and an investigator for the Anchorage D.A.'s office. You know him; you met him the last time you were over to the cabin. Kenneth Dahl?"

Abel was slow to answer. He looked at her, his eyes fixed on her face. "Yeah, I remember, I guess," he said, picking his words with care. "The Kennedy clone from Boston. More teeth than brains." He watched Kate redden with open satisfaction. "Why you looking for him? He owe you some money?"

Kate took a deep breath and held it. It was bad enough that she had introduced Kenneth Dahl to the Park in the first place, and why; she remembered Jack's last words to her the day before and cringed away from that "why." It was bad enough that her encouragement had led Ken to believe he knew his way around it, and its residents. It was worse that she knew he had come in after the ranger to prove a point to her. Ken had been missing more than two weeks, two weeks of record low temperatures and no snow. Letting Abel pick a fight over her love life would only delay Ken's being found that much longer. She exhaled slowly, and said in a mild voice, "You ever meet the ranger?"

"Might have," Abel said, looking disappointed. "They all look alike to me. What you want with him?"

"He's missing. Jack sent Ken in to look for him, and now Ken's missing, too. I'm going in for the Anchorage D.A., on loan to the FBI."

"The FBI?"

She grinned. "Don't look so nervous, Abel. So far as I know, the FBI still lets the Fish and Game handle out-of-season hunting violations. Yeah, the missing ranger's father is a U.S. congressman, and he got the FBI on it. Jack Morgan came to see me yesterday with one of J. Edgar's finest in tow."

Abel gave her a long, keen look. "Morgan, is it? How'd they come in? Nobody landed here yesterday."

She shook her head and warded off the offer of a Ding Dong with an inward shudder. Abel never ate anything that wasn't covered in sugar or deep-fried. "They drove to Ahtna and took a snow machine over the railroad tracks to Tana and then followed the old railroad grade to my place."

He raised one eyebrow. "Morgan better watch that shit with the tracks. Essy Beerbohm got himself run over last month by the Fairbanks train."

She winced. "I hadn't heard. Hauling supplies?"

"Yup."

"How is Cindy taking it?"

Abel's mouth turned down. "She moved in with Sandy Mike last week."

Kate looked at him and said, "Don't be so judgmental, Abel. It's not easy getting into a cold bed night after night."

Abel's spine stiffened and he glared at her. "I know that better than her, and come to think of it, better than you, too, girl."

Kate, already regretting speaking up in favor of a woman she'd never liked that much anyway, said hastily, "How about this cold spell?"

Abel, as all true Alaskans are by talk of the weather, was immediately diverted. "It's a bitch, ain't it? If it don't snow again pretty soon, spring runoff's going to be lousy. At this rate the creeks'll be running so low we won't see so much as a scale next spring, let alone a whole fish." He paused, and said, "This ranger, what'd you say his name was?"

"Mark Miller. You remember him?"

Abel considered. "I believe he just might be the fella I found in the Lost Wife this summer."

29

Kate looked at him, surprised. "What was he doing in that old widow-maker?"

"I asked him that," Abel replied, "just before I chased his ass down Shamrock Mountain with my twelve-gauge." Abel cocked his head. "He kept yelling something about the Lame Dog Lode."

Kate groaned gently. "I suppose whoever suckered him with that old chestnut sold him a deed to the Brooklyn Bridge, too."

"It don't matter. Someone was bound to try it on him, the way they do all the cheechakos." Abel gave a sardonic grin. "Offhand I'd say he don't care whether it's true or not, anymore. How long's he been gone?"

"About six weeks. Ken's been gone for two plus."

Abel snorted. "That ranger probably got drunk and fell into a snowbank on the way home from the Roadhouse." His teeth shut with a snap, and after a moment he said gruffly, "Sorry, girl."

She shook her head. "It's all right, Abel. That was my first thought. But now there's Ken gone, too." She gave him a tight smile and quoted one of his favorite sayings back at him. "Something smells and it ain't squaw candy."

He looked at her, his eyes narrowed. "Dahl the reason you're getting involved?"

She was silent for a moment. Then she sighed and drained her cup. "I took him into Niniltna last spring, let him sniff around, get familiar with the place," she said. Her voice rasped against her scarred throat. "And we did some hiking up around Copper City, some dip-netting in the Kanuyaq. He was learning the Park, and he would have said so back at work. Jack would figure he was the logical one to send. I feel...responsible."

Abel busied himself with the coffeepot. "'Responsible'?" He refilled her cup and then his. "You been shacked up with the guy off and on almost a year now, girl, and all you feel is 'responsible'?"

"I thought I'd start with my grandmother," Kate said through teeth she was trying hard not to clench. "She's sure to have met this ranger, and I introduced Ken to her so she's the first place he'd stop."

He nodded thoughtfully. "Good idea. She always knows everything that's going on in the Park. I swear the woman's like that Greek you used to read to me about, the one with the thousand eyes that was always watching you."

"Hundred eyes. Argus. Only the night has a thousand eyes, Abel."

"Argus," Abel said, unheeding. "Yeah, that's the guy. Well, you can't do better than talk to Ekaterina." He looked from her to Mutt, sitting next to him, watching the Ding Dong travel from plate to mouth and back again, yellow eyes unblinking. He grinned and tossed her a piece. Mutt caught it neatly and swallowed it in one gulp, and wagged her tail, hopeful for more. "Your teeth are going to rot in your head, dog," he told her, and said to Kate, "I suppose you figured on leaving the monster with me?"

"I might have," Kate said with a grin, "if I didn't know that five minutes after I left you'd have Balto knocking her up."

He heaved a mournful sigh, belied by the frosty twinkle in his eyes. "Girl, I swear I don't know who's been telling these lies about me."

She laughed and said, "You have, Abel, all my life."

"Get out of here," he told her, affronted.

"I have to," she said, gulping down the rest of her coffee and rising to her feet in one movement. "I'm going to stop in

31

to see Chick and Mandy on my way, and I'd better leave now if I want to make it into Niniltna this afternoon."

"Chick's in jail."

Kate paused in the act of zipping her jumpsuit. "What for this time?"

"I ain't saying nothing." Abel cleared his throat and shrugged. "But I heard tell it was more of the usual. Disturbing the peace. Drunk and disorderly. Resisting—"

"—arrest. Assaulting a police officer," Kate said, and sighed. "Where?"

"Anchorage."

"I thought Mandy had Chick restricted to the homestead this winter."

Abel opened his front door and looked lazily at the sky, eyes narrowed, basking in the weak sunlight. "Demetri Totemoff found her brand spanking new snow machine run into a ditch close to Tana."

"Hoo boy."

"Yup. So far, she's refused to make his bail."

• • •

Mandy Baker's homestead was large and sprawling and cluttered and looked unkempt even beneath the saving grace of winter snow. It was surrounded by birch trees, and to almost every narrow trunk was tethered a dog, and every dog was taking notice as Kate came down the trail. They whined, yelped, barked, yipped, growled, snarled and howled, hurling themselves against their harnesses, lips curled back from their teeth. Like Abel's pack they were all huskies or husky mix, and their tails curled over their rumps like so many vigorously waving ostrich plumes.

Kate pulled up and stopped the Super Jag five feet from one large, white, eager specimen, who promptly flung himself into a frenzy of slavering warning. Mutt jumped down from behind Kate, sniffed the air in his general direction, yawned, turned around three times, lay down and curled herself into a ball with her nose beneath her tail, and to all appearances fell asleep, inches from his snapping teeth. Affronted by this display of sangfroid, the huge canine hurled himself against the length of his chain and yapped hysterical threats of bloodletting and slaughter. Kate stepped around Mutt and cuffed him lightly on the jaw, whereupon he dropped to his belly as if felled by an axe handle and groveled ingratiatingly. "Calm down, Hardhead. Anybody'd think you hadn't seen a friend come down that path in years."

"He hasn't," a calm voice said behind her, and with a grin Kate turned.

"What's with him? You'd think I was a total stranger."

"Where do you think he got his name? He's not bright enough to recognize a friend," Mandy said dryly. "He's just barely bright enough to pull a sled."

"Not lead dog material," Kate suggested.

"Not hardly."

"You make up your mind to run in the Beargrease next month?"

Mandy shook her head. "I'm saving them up for the Iditarod in March."

Kate grinned. "Butcher's going to love to hear that."

Mandy grinned back. "Ah, she's not greedy, she's won four times. She'll figure it's my turn. Swensen might be a little annoyed, though. You know how he feels about women mushers."

She was a tall, lean, rangy woman, dressed in flannel shirt, jeans and boots that laced up to her knees. She had thick, straight, brown hair cut squarely around a face with big, strong bones, a structure that reminded Kate of a well-built cabin— sturdy, weatherproof and able to stand up to the worst winter storm. Her gray eyes were deeply set and shrewd and enveloped in wrinkles. The wrinkles were deceptive; Mandy was two years Kate's junior, and the wrinkles came from years of staring into an arctic sun low on the horizon, from the back of a dogsled on a long, cold trail that led everywhere but home.

"Come on in, Kate," she said. "I'm cleaning lamp chimneys. You can help."

"Oh goody," Kate said, following her inside.

"I'm almost done," Mandy assured her. "This is one job I never get a jump on. In winter it's dark all day and I keep the lamps lit from the time I get up until the time I go to bed. In summer the sun shines around the clock and it gets so bright I have to pull the shades and light the lamps anyway. I can't win." Without changing her inflection Mandy added, "When we're done in here, you can help me move Chick's stuff back into the cabin."

"Oh, Mandy."

The younger woman shook her head firmly. "He knows the rules. Sober, he sleeps with me. Drunk, he's out in the cold."

"Doesn't matter where his stuff is here when he's in jail in Anchorage," Kate observed in a mild voice. "How long has he been in now?"

"Fifteen days."

"When are you going to make bail for the poor bastard?"

"I've got to get his stuff moved first."

"Oh," Kate said, and added, "in that case I'll help you move it."

34

They worked in companionable silence for the twenty minutes it took to shift Chick's belongings, which consisted of a number of beer boxes filled with clothes that smelled strongly of dog, a battered transistor radio and a half-empty box of batteries, a grimy deck of playing cards, a set of carving tools, a walrus tusk with a cribbage board carved on one side, and every book ever written by Louis L'Amour. Afterward they relaxed over coffee and sandwiches in the lodge kitchen, a large, smoke-stained room in which it paid to be short, as pots and pans hung from the ceiling the way stalactites hung from the roof of a cave. "He wrecked my new snow machine, did you hear?"

"Uh-huh."

"I mean really wrecked it, Kate. It looks like he bounced it off every tree between here and Tana. The damn thing took most of my purse from last year's Yukon Quest." She chewed her last bite of sandwich and swallowed. "What really pisses me off is that he insists he didn't do it."

"Didn't get drunk and go to Anchorage?" Kate asked.

"No, he admits to that."

"And a good thing, too."

"Mmm. No, he says he didn't take the Polaris."

"What does he say happened?"

"That he hitched a ride with a couple of hunters in a Snowcat to Ahtna and took the train in from there."

"Uh-huh."

"Yeah, that's what I thought." Gray eyes surveyed Kate shrewdly. "What brings you down the road today?"

Kate looked down into her coffee cup. "Jack Morgan showed up yesterday morning, wanting me to look for a ranger who's been missing in the Park for six weeks." Mandy grunted. "Yeah, I know," Kate said, "but the kid's father is a congressman Outside and nudged the FBI. Their local rep knew Jack and he sent Ken Dahl after the kid. Now Ken's missing, too."

"Ken Dahl," Mandy said. "That the blond bombshell of Beacon Hill Dahl?"

"Yeah. Mark Miller's the ranger's name. You ever meet him?"

"Little guy, dark, too young, kind of an environmental Jerry Falwell?"

Kate smiled. "I don't know about the Falwell part, but the rest matches the description. What do you mean, too young? Too young for what?"

"Too young to tell everybody how to run the Park." Mandy's laugh was short and humorless. "He testified in favor of developing the Park before that House subcommittee in Niniltna in October."

"Say anything that might get him killed?"

Mandy shot her a reproachful look. "Come now, Kate. He's a ranger. He's been trained not to say much that wouldn't."

"Wonderful. What did he say, exactly?"

Mandy sat back in her chair and linked her hands behind her head. "Imagine the scene, if you will. The school gym, and Billy Mike's got it all tarted up in red, white and blue crepe paper. There's a long table set up on the stage, and a lectern facing it for the witnesses, and every folding chair in the Park unfolded on our brand new gym floor."

"Bet Bernie had a few things to say about that."

"Bet your ass. So all these Park rats get up and swear on their ancestors how the Park is their home and how improving the railroad grade into a real highway is going to ruin the quality of life for everyone and how the Alaska Railroad kills all those moose every winter and what makes this committee think a new road wouldn't be a danger to caribou migration, and so on and so on and so on. You get the general idea. Then Miller gets up, this intense little fucker from Outside, and contradicts everything that had been said before and actually has the gall to produce facts and figures, goddam statistics, can you imagine, to back up his theories. Yes, indeedy, he told us all how to run this here Park, like we'd never heard the words 'game management' put together in a sentence before."

Kate gave a sharp bark of laughter. "Mandy, the only game management you've ever been involved in is not getting caught when you run out of dog food and go caribou hunting in April. Between you and Abel I'm surprised there's anything left on four feet inside the Park."

Mandy grinned and for a moment looked like a little girl with her hand caught in the cookie jar. "Between you and me, so am I, Kate," she admitted. "Abel and me and the poachers."

"What poachers?" Kate said.

"Didn't Abel tell you?" Mandy said. "Couple weeks ago there was a whole hell of a lot of shooting going on up by the old Lost Wife Mine. It was calm that day and sound carried, you know the way it does in winter, and I heard it all. It wasn't me, and Abel told me it wasn't him, so..."

Kate said, amused, "He's got a haunch hanging from his cache right now."

"That old buzzard," Mandy said, disgusted. "You should have seen those big old blue eyes. 'Who me? Shoot game out of season?' And he thunders off all indignant. I actually felt bad about accusing him."

"Well," Kate said fairly, "it looks more the size of a moose haunch than a caribou, I'll give him that." She sighed, and said, "As for Miller, I hope you know you've just expanded my roster of suspects to include everyone in the Park."

"Surely not everyone," Mandy said.

"Give me a for instance."

"Abel," Mandy said with a straight face, and they both burst out laughing. When they sobered enough to be able to speak, Mandy said, "Did I tell you I knew Ken Dahl Outside?"

"No," Kate said, surprised. "In Massachusetts?"

"Uh-huh," Mandy said, grinning. "His family and mine were very close. In fact, Mother was kind of hoping for an alliance."

"She wanted you to marry him?"

"Back when she still thought I was going to graduate from Vassar and make my debut in a pink satin dress with a chiffon overskirt. I think she was hoping Ken would marry me, actually," Mandy said reflectively. "I think she thought he might be able to save me from L. L. Bean, where she and Dad had failed."

"He never told me. Were you tempted?"

"Nah. I was too involved with Robert Service at the time."

Kate laughed. "I'd like to meet your mother, Mandy. When are you going to break down and invite your folks up here?"

"Are you kidding? Mother thinks there are still buffalo in Buffalo."

"They've got to be proud of your racing."

Mandy shrugged. "If it doesn't happen on the track at Saratoga or offshore at Newport, it doesn't happen."

"Oh."

Later, standing in the doorway, she said, "Kate?"

Kate straddled her machine and looked up. "What?"

"What about Jack?"

The faint smile vanished from Kate's face. "What about him?"

"Did the temperature around here just drop sharply in the

last five seconds?" Mandy wondered aloud. "Maybe I should have said, What about you and Jack?"

"There is no me and Jack."

"Well, excuse me. I'm always making the mistake of believing what I see with my own eyes."

"It's a no go, Mandy," Kate said. "We don't agree on anything important."

"Kate," Mandy said, "it's important whether he puts the toilet paper on the roller to roll from the top or the bottom. The rest is ground rules and gravy."

"Easy for you to say," Kate grumbled, and fired up the Super Jag.

"Only because it's true," Mandy yelled after her.

CHAPTER 3

NINILTNA WAS A VILLAGE of eight hundred inhabitants that doubled in population in the summer when the salmon were running. This made it a metropolis by Alaskan bush standards. Its buildings crouched together on the flat, boggy muskeg at the edge of the Kanuyaq River—the river that served as the drainage ditch to the Park, the river into which all glaciers eventually melted and into which all creeks and streams flowed. It was the river up which the Chinook and sockeye and silver and humpy and dog salmon migrated to lay their eggs and die or to be tangled in set nets and air-freighted to Anchorage, there to be cleaned and frozen and shipped to restaurants and supermarkets half a world away. Usually the fishermen were Aleut and Athabascan and Tlingit Indians who fished with centuries-old squatters' rights. Occasionally a sports fisherman flew in, fished his limit and turned his catch over to one of half a dozen Native women who would filet it and smoke it, rendering it tough and stringy and delicious. It was said that smoked salmon was not real smoked salmon unless your jaw ached and your house smelled for a minimum of three days afterward.

Travel in Alaska is a matter of ceaseless caveats and cyclic qualifications. Thus the Kanuyaq River was navigable only as far as Niniltna, sixty-five miles upriver from its mouth on Prince William Sound, and then only by flat-bottomed riverboats or skiffs, and then only from the beginning of June until the end of September. By the first of November the river was frozen over; by December it was a crazy quilt of broken bergs. The townspeople crossed freely from bank to bank, and it stayed that way until breakup in March or April or, in years when winter outstayed its welcome, maybe even May.

Twenty, even ten years before, the town had been little more than a collection of shacks and the only building wired for electricity was the school. But in 1971 Congress passed the Alaska Native Claims Settlement Act. ANCSA settled forty million acres of land and a billion dollars on the six different ethnic groups of Alaska, ostensibly as compensation for the loss of lands historically occupied by their ancestors. The cynical saw it as a bribe to get the tribes to withdraw their objections to the construction of the TransAlaska Pipeline smack down the center of the state and, not coincidentally, all those Alaskan aboriginal hunting grounds.

Since that time, Niniltna's face had been radically altered. The town still had its percentage of two-by-four tar-paper shacks, heated by stoves made from fifty-five-gallon drums, but the majority of the buildings in Niniltna were now descended from a prefabricated lineage whose embryos were fertilized somewhere outside, usually in Seattle, after which they were shipped by SeaLand to Seward and via the Alaska Railroad to Anchorage. By then full-size modules, they were either trucked down the old railroad bed when the snow melted or barged up the river to Niniltna when the river ice melted in the spring. There they were borne into the full glory of single-story, tin-sided and tin-roofed American dream homes. Any extras were brought in by air, which was why an ordinary single-family dwelling in Niniltna could cost three times the price of a comparable dwelling in San Jose, California.

There isn't a lot of timber in Alaska outside of the Panhandle, and much of what is left barely gets thick enough through the trunk to use for fuel, let alone to employ in constructing a home. The prefab buildings were instantly identifiable by a uniform pale blue metal siding, and were all connected by a writhing mass of overhead wiring to the town's generator, in a building that produced an immense cloud of smoke which never completely dispersed in the still, frozen winter air.

There was one grocery store, where you could buy bananas for a dollar a pound and avocados for two dollars each. Both had been airfreighted in twice, once from Outside, the second time from Anchorage. The school was the only building with two stories, and its gym doubled as city hall, community center and, on occasion, jail. There was a landing just before the bend in the Kanuyaq, a broad sandy stretch where fishermen beached their boats to work on the hulls, stretched their nets for mending and, when the salmon were running, landed their fish. Just beyond this landing, Kate cut the engine of her snow machine and dismounted. She stood on a small rise in front of the beach and looked down on the tumble of buildings. She could have found her way around Niniltna blindfolded, in the dark. Today she could turn her back on it, and did.

Kate's grandmother's home, a loose, sprawling edifice which was most certainly not sided with blue tin, stood just yards from the stretch of beach. It had started out a tiny, one-room log cabin, made from anemic little birch and scrub spruce logs chinked with moss and river clay. This cabin had been added on to every ten years or so to encompass the ever larger generations of Moonins and Shugaks, and looked it. Over the rise of riverbank it hunkered down beneath a collection of roofs with differing pitches variously shingled with asphalt, cedar and split logs. It was surrounded by discarded fifty-five-gallon Chevron drums, Blazo boxes, old tires and odd lengths of lumber more precious than gold, which were never thrown away and if stolen could result in charges and countercharges of assault, if not murder.

At her side Mutt looked up at Kate inquiringly, her plumed tail curled up over her rump in a question mark. "Just because you've never been afraid of anything in your life doesn't mean I haven't been," Kate admonished her. Mutt cocked her head. "Sit," Kate said. Mutt squatted obediently, watching as Kate wiped her feet carefully on the doormat, squared her shoulders, lifted her chin and went in. The front door opened into a snow porch, which led directly into the house's all-purpose room, the kitchen.

Ekaterina Moonin Shugak sat where she'd always sat, in a chair backed up against the wall, between the oil stove and the kitchen table. Her hair was dark and skinned back into a bun. Her eyes were like Kate's, light brown and impenetrable at will. She had three chins and as many stomachs, and sat with her knees apart, her feet planted firmly on the faded and patched linoleum floor.

"So," she greeted her namesake. "Katya."

"Emaa." Kate bent down to kiss the surprisingly youthful skin of the old woman's cheek. "You look well."

"You would know that already if you chose to live at home among your own people."

Kate unzipped her snowsuit and sat down in the chair opposite her grandmother's, not replying. There wasn't any point in it; the argument was as old as she was, and Kate hadn't come here for a fight. She looked across the table, her face expressionless, her eyes calm.

The old woman was eighty years old as near as anyone had been able to figure, as even that traveling social security representative hadn't been able to get her to divulge her birthdate. And although no one with even the dimmest spark of self-preservation would ever dare insinuate that Ekaterina Moonin Shugak was growing senile, after eighty years some people tended to ideas that were fixed and immutable, and to hang on to them with their fingernails, teeth and toes. Kate reminded herself of this salient fact for the one thousandth time, and made what she hoped was a peace offering. "Is there cocoa?"

Her grandmother's stern expression lightened. She rose to her feet and moved deliberately to the stove, the floor creaking beneath her weight. Her back, Kate noticed, was as straight as it had ever been, her head as high, and as proud. She pulled the teakettle forward from the back of the stove, filled it at the sink and put it on to boil. From the shelf over the stove she took a cast-iron skillet and a large bowl covered with a dishcloth. She removed the cloth to reveal a mound of rising bread dough, and cut off a piece. She poured oil into the skillet and let it heat, rolled the remaining dough into loaves and put them in the oven. When the grease began to sputter she tore off chunks of the dough she had retained and fried it a golden brown on both sides. She put the pieces on a chipped plate and set it on the table with a cube of butter and a shaker of powdered sugar. By then the water was boiling. From a cupboard she took two mugs, a can of evaporated milk and a 48-ounce can of Nestle's Quik. She put three heaping teaspoonfuls of the powdered chocolate in each mug, punched holes in the can of milk and half filled the mugs, topping them off the rest of the way with boiling water. Steam rose and the smell of sweet chocolate mingled with the aroma of fried bread and made Kate's mouth water. Ekaterina reached for a spoon.

"Don't, emaa," Kate said, reaching for the mug, the first completely natural movement she'd made and the first completely natural words she'd spoken since arriving. "You know I like it lumpy." She took the spoon out of the mug, took a piece of fried bread from the plate, dipped it and took a bite, as absorbed in the right balance of cocoa to fried bread at thirty years of age as she had been at three. She smiled at the memory, and said around a mouthful of bread, "It's quiet here today, emaa. Where is everyone? Usually you're crawling with kids and supplicants."

Her grandmother blew on her cocoa and sipped it. "It's early, the kids are still in school. What's a supplicant?"

Kate grinned. "One who grovels in return for a favor."

"Oh." The old woman thought it over, and permitted a gratified smile to cross her face.

Kate's free hand sifted through the drift of papers on the kitchen table, and came up with a two-page document typed on legal-size paper. She read the first paragraph, read it a second time, and raised her eyes to look again at the old woman. "I thought this was a dead issue."

Ekaterina twitched the paper out of her granddaughter's hand and placed it out of reach. "Not quite. Not yet."

"I thought Billy and the rest of the council voted it down."

"They did," Ekaterina said, taking a sip of her cocoa with the air of a connoisseur.

Kate sighed. "Oh, emaa."

Her grandmother looked up. "You still think it's a joke?"

"Oh, no, emaa," Kate said, without the trace of a smile. "I don't think of it as a joke."

"What, then?"

Kate was silent in her turn. At last she said, "We invent so many prejudices on our own. Do we really need to impose new ones from the top down?" Ekaterina said nothing, and Kate said slowly, feeling her way, "Emaa, someday you are going to have to drag yourself, kicking and screaming if necessary, into this century. You want to keep the family at home, keep the tribe together and make the old values what they were." She leaned forward, her fists on the table, and spoke earnestly, looking straightly into eyes so like her own. "It's not going to happen. We have too much now, too many snow machines, too many prefabs, too many satellite dishes bringing in too many television channels, showing the kids what they don't have. There's no going back. We've got to go forward, bringing what we can of the past with us, yes, but we've got to go forward. It's the only way we're going to survive."

Ekaterina nodded, and Kate, exasperated, said, "I hate it when you do that. I talk myself blue in the face and you nod and smile and nod and smile, and then you go on and do whatever you were going to do in the first place. It's infuriating."

Ekaterina nodded and smiled, and Kate gave a reluctant smile. "You're impossible, emaa."

"What you mean is that I am almost as stubborn as you are, Katya."

Kate's smile faded. "Maybe that is what I mean." She drank her cocoa. "Emaa," she said, knowing she was wasting her time but unable to leave her argument unfinished, "if you persist on this course, you will divide the people in the Park. Only this time it won't be the greenies versus the strip miners and the lumberjacks, or the sports fishermen versus the commercial fishermen, or the Park rats versus Outsiders. This"—she indicated the paper—"this will split the races themselves, right down the middle. ANCSA was bad enough for the Anglos to reconcile themselves to. Some never have, and it's hard to blame them. They don't get quarterly dividends from Native associations, and can't take their kids to ANS for free medical care. And now you want tribal sovereignty? One law for us, another for them? Do you want to start a war?"

Her grandmother smiled, a long, slow smile, and refrained from nodding. "Perhaps only a little one," she said mildly. "Enough to wake up the Aleuts to their exploitation."

Kate raised her eyebrows. "'Exploitation'? Is that this month's new buzzword? And don't try that us-against-the-world, preserve-the-purity-of-the-race bullshit on me, emaa. Your great-great-grandfather was a hundred percent Russian cossack, your uncle was a Jewish cobbler who came north with the Gold Rush, and your sister married a Norwegian fisherman. We Aleuts are about as pure of ancestry as one of Abel's dogs." Before Ekaterina could reply Kate raised her hands palms out. "Okay. I'm sorry. Let's drop it. It's none of my business anyway. I will not let you suck me into this argument again." She fortified herself with a gulp of cocoa and choked over a lump. "I'm here because I need a favor myself, emaa," she said.

"You are a supplicant," Ekaterina stated, with a faint smile.

Kate couldn't help grinning. "I guess I am. I'm looking for someone. Two someones. One of them was a new ranger for the Park; he'd been here about six months before he went missing. His name was Mark Miller, Anglo, small, thin, dark hair, hazel eyes, twenty-one years old. Have you met him?"

Her grandmother took another sip of her cocoa and sat for a moment, not speaking. "Mark Miller," she said at last, mouthing the name as if it spoiled the taste of her drink. Her eyelids were lowered, hiding her eyes. She looked almost asleep, and only thirty years of personal experience kept Kate from thinking she was.

The room was warm, and Kate unbuttoned the top buttons of her shirt. The kettle steamed on the back of the stove, the smell of baking bread teased her nostrils, the early afternoon sun sent thin, searching tendrils through the windows, and her grandmother was taking too long to answer.

"Did you know him?" Kate probed, not changing her relaxed position but alert for every word, every movement her grandmother might make. She liked this job less and less with every passing moment, but Ken was missing and it was her fault. No. She gave herself a mental shake. He was a grown man, and she had never minimized the dangers of the Park and its inhabitants, be they on four legs or two, which not least dangerous of the two-legged variety was the old woman sitting across from her now. She jumped when Ekaterina at last decided to speak.

She spoke slowly, deliberately, as if remembrance of the events were coming to her as she talked. "Xenia was seeing some young Outsider a month or two ago."

"What was his name?"

The old woman shrugged, her eyes on the strong, wrinkled hands wrapped around her mug.

Kate said patiently, "Was it Miller, emaa?"

There was a long silence, and then the old woman said, "It might have been."

Kate's mind was busy creating and discarding scenarios. "A month or two, that fits. He hasn't been heard from in six weeks." Kate looked keenly at the old woman. "So he was seeing Xenia, was he?"

"Yes." Her grandmother did not elaborate, and from her manner Kate knew she had said her last word on the subject.

"Well," Kate said, "I guess the next step is to find Xenia and talk to her."

"You said you were looking for two people."

"Yes," Kate said. "The ranger's family has pull in Washington, D.C. They put the FBI on it."

"The FBI?"

Kate laughed. "You look just like Abel did when I told him the FBI was on the trail, emaa."

The old woman became, if possible, even more deliberate in speech. "Abel?"

"Yeah, have either of you robbed any banks lately? Anyway, the local agent asked Jack Morgan if he would look into it since he knew the Park, and he sent Ken Dahl out here." She paused with her mug halfway to her lips, and her smile faded. "He's been missing for two weeks."

"The blond man," her grandmother said. "I remember. You brought him to the potlatch this summer."

Kate stiffened. "Yes, emaa, I brought him to the potlatch, and I have yet to hear the end of it." Her grandmother looked bland, and Kate smacked her mug down on the table and said explosively, "It was only a party, for God's sake; it's not some holy tribal ceremony. I brought Jack—" Her mouth snapped shut, and she wondered bitterly what it was about her grandmother that could put her so instantly on the defensive.

"For the four years before that, yes, I remember him, too. Jack Morgan. A good man."

"For an Anglo and an Outsider," Kate agreed sarcastically. "Yes, I know."

The two women were silent, listening to the kettle whistle on the stove. "Katya," the old woman said at last, "I have a favor to ask you now."

With Ekaterina, there was always a quid pro quo. Nothing

was for free, not even for granddaughters anointed to follow in her footsteps. Perhaps especially not those, Kate thought. "What?" she said. "Another council meeting you feel I should attend? Another amendment to the Native association charter you feel it necessary I be present to vote for in person?" The old woman looked at her, and she looked away. "Sorry, emaa," she said gruffly. "I didn't mean to be rude."

"I want you to talk to Xenia, Katya," her grandmother said.

"I'm going to anyway, but what do you want me to say to her?"

"She wants to move to town."

Kate's shoulders slumped a little. It was always the same whenever she came home. It was one of the reasons she rarely did. In Ekaterina's view, Kate was the elder sister of her family and Ekaterina's personal sergeant at arms. It was, Ekaterina believed, one of Kate's duties to mount a guard on the perimeter of the jail in case any of her cousins' kids took it into their heads to escape the confines of family, village and park. Escapes went on all the time, some successful, some thwarted. "And I'm supposed to talk her out of it?"

"She wants you to find her a job. You won't."

Kate took a deep breath, and expelled it. "I might. If she's really sincere about it, and willing to work, I might look for something for her to do. Maybe even in the D.A.'s office."

"You will do no such thing."

Kate met her grandmother's stern eyes. "Why not?" she said. "What's all that wrong with Anchorage?"

"Why did you leave it?" the old woman countered, and Kate flushed.

"What is there for her to do here?" she snapped. "Get pregnant so she can go on welfare? And then she needs more money so she has another baby, and then she needs more so she has another? Or maybe she could marry some guy from Tana who didn't finish high school, who fishes all summer and drinks all winter and beats on her in between? And then he drinks too much to fish and she goes on welfare anyway and gets Bernie to cash her checks for her, and maybe because she's lonely, or maybe because she just wants time off from the kids she starts drinking herself, and spending her weekends at the Roadhouse, leaving the kids to raise themselves, until one night she staggers out for a leak in the snow and passes out and dies of exposure? Is that what you want for her?" The last words were almost shouted, and Kate stood, glaring at her grandmother, breathing hard.

"Xenia is not your mother," Ekaterina said softly into the angry silence of her kitchen.

They stared at each other. Kate looked away first. "Ah, the hell with it."

Ekaterina allowed the silence to linger, for Kate to lose steam, and then she said softly, her words dropping quietly into the silence, "It was easy for you, Katya. It would not be so easy for Xenia."

Easy? Kate looked at Ekaterina and laughed; she couldn't help herself. For a change Ekaterina looked off-balance. It was a bitter and entirely unamusing sound, Kate's laughter, and Kate let it die a natural death. She paced once around the room, her hands shoved in her pockets. "I went Outside last year, did I tell you? Jack has an interest in an apple orchard in Arizona. We rented an RV and drove everywhere. Beautiful country. Not like Alaska, but beautiful in its own way."

"Sounds like fun," Ekaterina said neutrally, alert to the seeming change of subject, watching her granddaughter with wary eyes.

"Mmm. One day, while we were driving everywhere, we came to a Indian gift shop by the side of the road, and we stopped. The man who was running it, a Navajo he said when we asked him, wanted to know where we were from. We told him, and he wanted to know, where do Indians live in Alaska? Jack said, a lot of the time next door. He didn't believe us. I told him I was an Aleut, and he looked at Jack, and he looked at me, and he looked at our camper van, and he looked at my clothes, and he didn't say anything, but it was obvious he didn't believe that, either."

Ekaterina chuckled, and Kate smiled. "I know. So we showed him pictures of where we lived, and he laughed. He wanted to know what kind of reservations we had, and we told him, none, or none like they do Outside. He still wouldn't believe us, but he was too polite to call us liars to our face, and so he sold me this gorgeous silver bracelet and took us home for supper."

Kate stopped next to the stove, her hands held out over it. "Home was a twenty-year-old Airstream trailer propped up on bricks and insulated with newspapers, sitting next to a dry creek bed. No power, no running water, but the creek ran most of the year, he told us. His oldest girl was thirteen. She was pregnant. They wanted to know about Alaska and we had a map and showed it to them, and they couldn't read enough to understand it. His wife was drunk from the moment we stepped into his trailer, and before we left her sister and her sister's husband showed up with another bottle. It was a school day, but none of the kids had bothered to attend. What was the point? He asked us. There were no jobs on the reservation."

The old woman looked at her, one arm on the table, the other planted on a knee, her face impassive, and Kate said gently, "They stay home, emaa. They never leave it. And do you know who they have for tribal police? The FBI. There's your self-determination. There's your sovereign nation. Don't you see, that by forcing Xenia to stay here, you would be forcing her to give up any chance she has at a future?"

Ekaterina sat still, again her eyes half-closed. She said, "Billy Mike was in Prudhoe last year when the Barrow whalers landed that bowhead. They were not in kayaks, they were in Zodiacs with outboard motors. Their harpoons had exploding heads. One of the oil companies provided a tractor with a come-along and winched the whale ashore, after the hunters had struck three times and finally killed it. A third of the meat was ruined by the time the carcass was beached. Another third spoiled before it could be harvested, before even the polar bears could gather to finish it off, the way they were put here to do. This is your twentieth century, Katya. This is your civilization. Don't you see that if Xenia leaves, she abandons the culture that gave her birth?"

Kate smiled at the old woman, and flicked the switch next to the door, plunging the room into arctic afternoon gloom. "And yet you have electricity in your house, emaa. You have running water in your kitchen and bathroom."

"Provided by the association for its members," Ekaterina said composedly.

Kate flicked the switch again, restoring the light. "Funded by taxes on Prudhoe Bay oil, emaa."

CHAPTER 4

UNFORTUNATELY KATE KNEW EXACTLY where to find her cousin Xenia.

Bernie's Roadhouse was twenty-seven miles away from Niniltna, which put it exactly nine feet, three inches outside the Niniltna Native Association's tribal jurisdiction. A road of sorts, following the west bank of the Kanuyaq River, connected the two. It was a road created and maintained from the wear and tear of truck tires and snow-machine treads. Any other road with that much traffic would have qualified for federal matching funds.

The bar was a low, sprawling place built of the inevitable plywood and two-by-fours flown in piece by prohibitively expensive piece, strapped to the struts of a Super Cub whose young pilot paid off the loan on his plane with that job. A satellite dish hung precariously from the eaves. There was a shack for the generator, another for the water tank whose contents Bernie pumped out of the Kanuyaq each fall, and the house in which Bernie and his wife, Enid, born a Shugak, and seven children lived and from which Bernie fled nightly into the Roadhouse. A half dozen tiny cabins, where Bernie put his children to work as soon as they were tall enough to change sheets on a bed, were rented out year-round to the stray tourists and Demetri Totemoff's hunting parties.

Unfinished wooden steps climbed up to the front door.

Inside, the building was one cavernous square fifty feet on a side, with exposed beams that patrons occasionally swung from, depending on how late the hour and when Bernie cut them off. A bar with stools and a brass foot rail ran down the left side of the room, with a mirror and racks of dusty bottles of exotic liqueurs in back of it. There was a large television hanging from one corner of the ceiling, with tall men chasing a basketball across the screen. Tables and chairs, video games and a jukebox with selections guaranteed to be not more than five years old filled up the rest of the room. There were two restrooms, with functional toilets, and homesteaders for miles around came just to remember how it felt not to have to hang it out in the cold with the mosquitoes snapping at your ass in the summer and the dogs doing the same thing in the winter. On New Year's Eve and on the Fourth of July the bar stayed open until five, three hours past its usual closing time, and on such occasions Bernie had been known to bring in live entertainment from as far away as Tok.

The room hadn't been swamped out in memory of man, and it smelled strongly of stale cigarette smoke and vomit. Behind the bar was Bernie, tall, dark and skinny, with a calm face and a hairline that was marching inexorably up the crown of his head. The remainder was clipped back into a ponytail, a defiant reminder of those halcyon days when he had been more hippy and less yuppy and much, much younger.

It was noisy that night, like every other night. Mutt saw Bernie and bounded across the room to jump up with her two front paws on the bar.

"Hey, no dogs allowed in—Oh, it's you, Mutt," Bernie said. "Hold on a minute." He turned and plucked a package of beef jerky off a stand and ripped it open. He tossed a chunk to Mutt, who caught it neatly in her teeth. Bernie looked between her ears and said, "Hey, Kate." Stretching out a thin, wiry hand, he added, "It's been a while."

"Not long enough," she said, taking his hand and shaking it warmly.

He gave an exaggerated wince and examined his hand tenderly. "You been splitting too many logs, Kate."

"You haven't been practicing your slam dunks, Bernie."

"What'll you have?"

"Coke," she said.

"Damn," he said, reaching for a tall glass, "you're bad for business, Kate. I never make any money off you."

"You do when you charge a buck and a half for a Coke," she said, digging in her pocket.

He waved her money away and leaned on the bar, his arms folded in front of him. She sipped her Coke and looked around. The smoke obscured her vision, and the bass from the jukebox was powerful enough to bounce her right off her stool. The talk was necessarily loud, the dancing energetic and the drinking nonstop. "You're not doing too bad," she said, half-smiling.

"Mmm. I should do all right if I can keep Billy Mike and that bunch off my back."

"You having problems with the tribal council again?"

"Nah." Bernie grinned. "I've been allowed a few months' grace, seeing's how the boys' team brought the state championship home last March."

"For the second time in four years."

Bernie grinned and said nothing.

"How's the team shaping up this year?"

He shrugged. "Too soon to tell." Bernie never handicapped the teams he coached.

Suzy Moonin came up to the bar, said hello to Kate and ordered a rum and Coke. Bernie looked at her and shook his head gently but with finality. "No, Suzy."

Suzy, a plump young woman with sparkling brown eyes and punked hair tucked behind her ears, said blankly, "What?"

He met her eyes squarely. "You're pregnant. I don't serve expectant mothers."

She flushed. "Who told?"

"Your mother was in last night."

"That bitch!" she spat.

"True," he admitted. "Doesn't make any difference. You're cut off until after the baby's born. Would you like a Coke? Or maybe a Shirley Temple? I'll put in an extra cherry."

She stared at him impotently, her body rigid with anger. Then she reached over and slapped the glass he was polishing out of his hand. It crashed to the floor in a hundred pieces, and she swung around and stamped across the room.

"Someone'll share," Kate said.

Bernie sighed and started picking up glass. "Probably. If I catch them at it I'll throw the both of them out."

"Why don't you just throw her out now?"

"If she wants it bad enough, she'll find it."

"Why don't you just close up shop, then?"

Bernie sighed again. "Don't go getting sanctimonious on me, Kate. I may be the only game in town but when they lay down three bucks I give them three bucks' worth of booze. That bootlegger you busted last winter was getting forty bucks for a bottle of Windsor Canadian that would cost seven in Anchorage. Thanks for that, by the way. Didn't get a chance to say so, afterwards."

Kate couldn't argue with him because she knew he was right. "Get any more CARE packages from your folks?"

He brightened. "Funny you should ask. Got one on today's mail plane." He stooped to lift a large, cardboard U-Haul box from beneath the counter. Kate knelt on the stool so she could peer in. "Water filter? Waterproof compass? Hey, a Swiss army knife! Does it have a screwdriver?"

He recovered the knife deftly. "Straight-edge and Phillips."

"Wow."

"Forget it. Buy your own."

"What's this? Mutt, get out of the light!" This as Mutt's large head appeared over the side of the box to peer in, too. She gave Kate a wounded look and jumped back down on the floor. "Vitamins? Doesn't your mom think you eat right?"

"She doesn't think blubber can be all that nutritious as a dietary staple."

Kate looked at Bernie's poker face, and he added, "And she wants to know if all my Eskimo friends live in igloos." He pulled a down sleeping bag out of the CARE package and displayed it.

Fascinated, Kate said, "What'd she say when you told her you'd never met an Eskimo or seen an igloo, and that muktuk was in short supply since whales got put on the endangered species list, and that Aleuts eat seal muktuk anyway?"

"I didn't tell her." Bernie grinned.

Kate looked at the box, her brow puckered. "Your mom and your sisters keep sending you all this stuff. What's your dad say?"

Bernie's grin vanished. "Nothing. At least not to me."

She decided to chance it. "Why not?"

Bernie was still for a moment. He relaxed and sighed, and even laughed a little. "Oh hell. I was a regular flower child, Kate, and he was regular Army. I got beat up at Chicago in '68, I danced in the mud at Woodstock in '69, and I burned

58

my draft card on the steps of the Capitol in '70, just before I left for Canada. He, on the other hand, put his public service time in at Anzio, Arnhem and Bastogne." Bernie made a wry face. "Neither of us ever let the other one forget it."

"I thought you said he doesn't talk to you."

"Or me to him. That's how we never forget it." He looked past her. "Damn."

She swiveled, to see Suzy sipping from a glass. She put it down hastily when she saw them watching her. She tossed her head and pulled Mickey Kompkoff out onto the dance floor. "Who's the father, do you know? Of Suzy's baby?"

"You have been out of touch. She married Mickey last month."

"Oh Christ no," Kate said, casting an involuntary look over her shoulder. "Tell me you're kidding."

"Nope." He shook his head. "We all tried to stop her. She wouldn't listen. I think she decided anything was better than living at home with her mother and that parade of uncles."

Kate wanted to cry. She'd gone to school with Suzy's older sister, and she remembered the days when Suzy had tagged along behind the two older girls, begging to be included in their games. She changed the subject. "Listen, Bernie, I'm looking for someone, a park ranger, name of Mark Miller. He ever been in here?"

Bernie grinned. "Everyone comes to Bernie's."

Kate gave an elaborate shudder. "Please. You ever meet him?"

"Yeah."

"To remember?"

"Yeah, sure I remember him. Who could forget?"

"Why? What made him so special?"

"Oh, hell, Kate, you know the type." She looked a question

and he elaborated. "Sierra Club commando. Fresh out of college, knew the Latin names for every animal, vegetable and mineral in the Park, could quote verbatim from both Johns."

"Both Johns?"

Bernie grinned. "Muir and McPhee. And sometimes Izaak Walton, but I think he'd quote Walton only when he wanted to really piss off old Sam Dementieff, or any other commercial fisherman he could find."

She laughed. "That bad?"

He shrugged and wiped the bar. "He was an okay kid. A little wet behind the ears, but you could tell he really loved the Park. Wanted to open it up and share it with the whole world, as long as the world didn't have a pickax or a rifle or a fishing pole in its hand." Bernie polished a glass in silence, and then said in an altered voice, "It was kind of nice, actually."

"What was?"

"All that enthusiasm, you know?" Bernie looked up. "He really did care, Kate. I remember one time he came in here and got about half-swacked and pulled out a copy of the congressional act that made Yellowstone a national park." He grinned. "And I hear tell he had a poster of Teddy Roosevelt on the wall of his office at Park Headquarters."

"You liked him," Kate said. She was a little surprised that Bernie, committed by inclination and profession to the industrial development of the Park, would speak well of a bona-fide, dyed-in-the-wool, card-carrying greenie.

Bernie shrugged and hung the glass by its stem from the overhead rack. "Made a change from the usual rape, pillage and plunder boys."

"Did I hear someone call my name?" A burly man with a red face and short, stiff red hair that stood straight out all over his head pushed in next to Kate. Mutt gave a warning grumble, deep in her throat, and subsided reluctantly when Kate laid a reassuring hand on her head.

"Hello, Mac," Bernie said. "What'll it be?"

"The usual. Hello, Kate, what brings you into the Park? Haven't seen you for months."

"Just visiting, Mac. What are you doing here in the middle of winter? You figured out a way to dredge a frozen creek?"

Mac laughed heartily. He was incapable of laughing any other way. He had sharp brown eyes that he made look merry when it suited him, and a stubborn chin he hid behind a hearty, good ol' boy hee-haw that disarmed those who didn't know him well, but put the few who did on full alert.

"Well, Kate," Mac said, "I'll tell you what I'm doing here, and maybe you'll put in a good word for me with Ekaterina. I want to lease the old Nabesna Mine off the association and put it into year-round production."

She raised her eyebrows. "You think you can make money year-round?"

Bernie set a Bud and a glass down in front of Mac and retired to the other end of the bar. Mac ignored the glass and lifted the bottle to his lips to chug half the liquid down. Some of it ran out of the sides of his mouth, and he smacked the bottle down on the bar and wiped his face on the sleeve of his shirt. "By damn, now that's what a thirsty man needs after a hard day in the mines! Bernie!" he hollered.

Bernie made his leisurely way back to where they were sitting, checking to see that the drawer to the cash register was closed, taking an occasional swipe with the bar towel at any available surface. Kate watched his slow progress with a hidden smile. Mac fidgeted impatiently. "Yeah, Mac?"

"Whyn't you get some draft in here, son? Some draft Bud, maybe. They support the America's Cup now, don't they?"

"I wouldn't know. I don't play tennis," Bernie said blandly. "And I've told you a hundred times, Mac, draft beer is too expensive to airfreight in."

Mac laughed heartily. "Can't be too awful goddam more expensive than what you're charging for this bottled crap, of which," he said, noisily finishing off the remainder of the bottle in front of him, "I'll have another and pronto."

Bernie served him and then drifted back down to the end of the bar to resume his interrupted conversation with Marvin Dementieff, just as Marvin gracefully abandoned the vertical for the horizontal and spent the rest of the evening curled up beneath the bar, a peaceful smile on his face, a gentle snore on his lips. Bernie searched Marvin's pockets for his keys and hung them on a board in back of the bar.

"So you want to open the mine year-round, Mac," Kate prodded. "You figure on making a profit at it?"

Mac drank beer. "Gold's up to almost four-fifty an ounce," he said, burping. "On my claims I could make money with a leaky pan and a broken pickax."

"You can't run a dredge with a frozen water supply, though," Kate said. "In fact, didn't I hear something about you not running the mine at all after you got yourself slapped with an injunction prohibiting further mining because you were messing up Carmack Creek?"

The burly man's brow darkened. "Ah, that little prick ranger. Yeah, he slowed me up some."

"Ranger?" Kate said. She found her glass motionless halfway to her lips, and raised it for another sip. "What ranger?" Mac's history passed in quick mental review, and she looked over at the man sitting next to her with new eyes.

Everyone in the Park knew where Mac Devlin came from and where he was going. Mac made sure of it. He was a mining engineer, had wanted to be a mining engineer, he said whenever he got the chance, since growing up in Butte, Montana, son of another mining engineer, who had put him through school and then kicked him out of the house. "Go find your own pay dirt and make your own money," his father said, "because I'm planning on spending all of mine before I die." That suited Mac, he reassured everyone. He didn't understand why all parents didn't kick their kids out early on. When he had his, he certainly would. On more than one occasion Kate had refrained from pointing out that with Mac as a father, in all probability when the time came, his kids would already be long gone.

Eventually Mac had hooked up with British Petroleum, who put him to work in oil fields all over the world and finally in Alaska, where he helped define the Prudhoe Bay super-giant oil field after the discovery well came in November 1968. The next year he was plotting a right-of-way for the pipeline haul road when his boss came up behind him and tapped him on the shoulder. "We're outa here, Mac."

"What?"

"The federal government's stopped the pipeline until they satisfy environmental concerns and native claims." His boss sighted on a piece of drill pipe and spat disgustedly.

When Nixon signed the TransAlaska Pipeline Act in 1973 and got the pipeline project back on track, there were resident environmentalists crouched protectively over every foot of prospective pipe-laying. It was almost more than Mac Devlin could bear, but the money was so good he stuck with it until pipeline construction was complete in 1977, when he told Alyeska Pipeline Service Corporation, his current employer, to go piss up a rope, took his savings and bought out some marginal gold mining claims in the Park. He fought off the depredations of d-2, the Alaska National Interest Lands Conservation Act of 1980, to maintain a going concern and retired Outside to wait for the price of gold to come back up.

It had, eventually, and now Mac Devlin was back in the Park, agitating for permission to expand his operations. He refused to hire locally, he bought his supplies in Seattle, he even flew his employees Outside for their R-and-Rs, all of which made him less than popular with the people of Niniltna. Mac's miners were the main reason for the presence of the baseball bat behind the bar of the Roadhouse, as well over half the fights there began between a MacMiner and any local who happened to be (a) out of work and (b) present.

Passing all this under rapid review, Kate said casually, "I thought it was the EPA who stopped your operation."

"Yeah, it was, but that little prick Miller was who turned me in. If I ever catch up to him, I'm going to take him outside and see how high he can bounce."

"That may be difficult, Mac."

Mac laughed heartily. "Have you seen that little prick, Kate?"

"No," she said. "Nobody has, for the last six weeks. He's gone missing. You wouldn't happen to know where, would you?"

"Missing? The hell you say." And then the intent of the rest of her words hit him. Mac said slowly, his eyes narrowing, "Why would I know anything about some punk ranger being missing?"

Kate shrugged. "Just a passing question." She met his eyes, and said softly, "Have you got an answer for me?"

Mac stared at her, his brown eyes lacking their usual veneer of merriment. "What are you doing here, Kate?" he said, his voice very soft.

"I'm looking for the little prick ranger, of course," she said calmly. "And for the Anchorage D.A.'s investigator that came up here looking for him two weeks ago. He's missing, too."

Mac said nothing. Kate kept her face impassive.

It was at that moment she became aware of a distant rumbling. Noise in the bar died down as others became aware of it, too. The ground began to shake and rumble in a rhythmic fashion. "Earthquake?" Kate called to Bernie.

"I don't think so," he started to say, but "Earthquake!" someone else screamed, and the rest was madness. Half a dozen people jammed themselves in the doorway, all of them trying to get through it at the same time, blocking exit to the thirty or so other patrons yelling and shoving ineffectually behind them. Bernie hotfooted it down to the end of the bar and looked out the window. "I thought so," he said, and had to shout it again to make Kate hear him over the yells of alarm filling the room. "It's not an earthquake. Look."

Kate, seeing that there was no way past the bodies that jammed the doorway, shrugged and came to peer over his shoulder.

Drawing up outside the Roadhouse was a bright yellow D-9 Caterpillar tractor. It had tracks over two feet wide and weighed about thirty tons and, with its 250-horsepower engine, had a top speed of six to seven miles an hour. Six to seven miles an hour pushing Mt. St. Elias in front of it, that is. It was standard operating equipment for excavations on the TransAlaska Pipeline. Mac Devlin had tried to get a permit to operate one in the Park. His application had been rejected with a reply so blistering that he had immediately burned it, and it took Dan O'Brian three whole days to get his hands on a copy out of Juneau so he could post it on the Trading Post bulletin board in Niniltna for the enjoyment of all.

The D-9 in front of the Roadhouse, wearing the proud insignia of the Alyeska Pipeline Service Corporation and apparently going every six or seven miles of its top speed, rumbled down the road, knocked over a scrub spruce, squashed Bernie's blueberry patch flat and lurched over the snow berm at the side of the parking lot, where, surrounded by open space for the first time in fifty miles, it became confused and started going around in a circle. The right side of the enormous blade sideswiped a parked truck, caving in the passenger side door, ripping off the front bumper and puncturing the left front tire. Shrieks were heard from beneath the truck's canopy. The door of the canopy swung up and a disheveled Betty Jorgensen dropped out of the back of the truck, followed by an equally disheveled Dandy Mike hauling up his pants. There was a furious yell from one of the onlookers. Bernie winced and groaned.

"Bill Jorgensen?" Kate said sympathetically, and Bernie nodded in a hopeless sort of way.

When the Cat finally ground to a halt, the doors on both sides of the cab popped open as if propelled by a small explosion. Two men fell out into the parking lot. One of them regained his feet; the other stayed on his hands and knees. Both of them were making a straight line for the Roadhouse. Kate and Bernie turned as one to watch the door. The stampede of bar patrons reversed course, giving plenty of house room to the two Cat skinners, as the one on his feet was brandishing a pistol.

"Probably isn't loaded," Bernie remarked.

"I wanna tequila sunrise and I want it now," the gunman said loudly, and shot a round into the roof for emphasis.

"Probably not," Kate agreed.

Bernie frowned at her repressively before he turned

to address the gunslinger. "Looks as if you've already had a few, friend."

The man peered at him through an alcoholic fog. "You Bernie?"

"The same."

The gunman surveyed the silent, terrified crowd and said plaintively, "What the fuck you running here, Bernie, a A.A. meeting? Gimme a drink!"

Bernie said, still in that flat, calm voice, "You've had a few too many already, friend."

The gunslinger swung around to look at his companion, who by now was up off all fours and peering owlishly over the head of an inflatable rubber doll. The doll had long blond hair and amazing proportions, and he clutched her firmly to his breast. "You hear that, Otis?" the man with the gun demanded. "Man says we can't have a drink."

Otis blinked once, slowly, and burst into tears.

The gunslinger turned back to wave his gun accusingly under Bernie's nose. "See that?" he demanded. "You made Otis cry! I orta shootcha!" He swayed closer and whispered confidentially, "Can't we have just one for the road? Otherwise Otis is gonna cry all the way home, and I just can't stand it."

Kate quivered and Bernie's hand clamped down hard on her wrist. "Nope. Not even one. Sorry."

The gunslinger scratched his head with the pistol barrel. "Well, shit." He stood in silence for a moment, his gaze wandering around the bar, taking in the crowd gathered in groups next to the wall like so many rabbits frozen by a car's headlights, noses twitching, eyes staring, afraid to move in any direction for fear of being run over or, in this instance, shot. The gunman surveyed them with a gathering disapproval. He leaned toward Bernie again and said in a whisper loud enough to be heard in Niniltna, "Listen, Bern ole buddy, no offense, but this don't look like a fun party anyway. We—Otis, stop that goddam bawling or I'll shoot your girlfriend."

Otis sobbed harder. Over the sobbing Kate heard a deep whap-whap-whap sound growing steadily louder outside the Roadhouse. She looked at Bernie out of the corner of one eye and saw him give a tiny nod.

The noise got louder and louder until the building was vibrating on its foundations and even Otis could hear it. There was another concerted rush for the outdoors. Kate turned toward the window in time to see a Bell Jet Ranger touch down next to the D-9 Cat.

"It's the trooper from Tok!" someone yelled, followed by a mixed chorus of cheers and boos. The roar of the helicopter's engine wound down to a high-pitched whine and the blades slowed. The door of the machine opened slowly.

"Behold," Kate cried, her low, raspy voice joyous, "the god in the machine!" Bernie gave her a vicious pinch and she tried to pull herself together.

Jim Chopin had been hired by the Alaska State Troopers before the height requirement was eliminated, and he got out of his helicopter, and kept coming out, and kept coming out, and kept coming out, until all of his five-foot-twenty-two-inch height was on the ground and upright. If there had been a weight requirement he would have passed that, too. As more than one Park denizen could testify, all two hundred and sixty pounds of him was muscle. As Billy Mike had been heard to say, "When Jim Chopin gets done climbing out of that helicopter, you know The Law has arrived."

The trooper wore a dark blue jacket over a light blue uniform shirt and dark blue pants with a gold stripe running up the outside seam of each leg. A flat-brimmed hat with a round crown sat low over his forehead, and the gold cord tied round the crown came to rest in two tassels centered perfectly over his nose. He wore a pistol in a black leather holster strapped to his right hip. He moved slowly, surely, with a regal presence so self-assured it was almost but not quite arrogant.

He strode through the door of the Roadhouse as if he owned the earth. The pipeliner with the pistol swung his arm in a perfect arc, so that the muzzle of the pistol came to rest on the trooper's forehead, directly between his eyes, centered perfectly below the two gold tassels.

Every eye, be it fascinated, horrified or approving, was fixed on the scene with equal intensity. For a moment no one moved or spoke. Then the trooper's deep, calm voice came clearly to them all. Directing his level gaze past the pistol and pistol holder, he addressed Bernie in a deep, calm voice. "What seems to be the problem here?"

There was one more moment of tense silence, and then the pipeliner sighed. "Oh fuck. It's Chopper Jim."

"Who?" Otis said.

"The goddam trooper, you drunken bum. Now what're we gonna do?"

The trooper stood motionless. The gunslinger's eyebrows met in a single busy bar above his eyes, which were unfocused; he was intent on the mental working out of some weighty problem. At last he leaned toward the trooper, the pressure of the gun muzzle against the trooper's forehead indenting the flesh, and said, "Listen, Chopper, how many years'm I gonna get for pulling a gun on you? 'Cause, if it's life, I might's well shootchya, dontchya think?"

The trooper's voice was deep and soothing. "I don't know, Davey, I think we could get it down to ten years or so, with time off for good behavior."

The gunslinger considered this. "Would they put me in with Otis?"

The trooper shrugged as much as he thought wise with a pistol at his head. "Why not?"

"You hear that, Otis? Three squares and a bed and no more welding outside at fucking ten below."

Otis plucked at Davey's sleeve and whispered. "Oh. Chopper, Otis wants to know if he can bring Cherry there with him."

"I don't see why not."

"Such a deal." Davey dropped his arm, tossed the trooper his pistol and a blinding smile. "Fuck 'em if they can't take a joke," he added, and barfed his dinner, a fifth of Absolut, three quarts of popcorn and two light beers down the front of the trooper's immaculate uniform pants.

About that time half a dozen Alyeska Pipeline security guards roared up on snow machines and were all over the Roadhouse like a swarm of angry bees. They were full of energy in spite of their all-afternoon cross-country excursion, and it was obvious that the only thing standing between the two prisoners and a distillation of some of that energy was Chopper Jim's calm, level gaze. The two pipeliners, drunk but not entirely stupid, themselves demonstrated a reverence for the Alaska Department of Public Safety in general and a touching affection for this representative in particular. It became necessary for them to be restrained; indeed, they displayed a distressing tendency to grasp at Chopper's Jim's large frame with hands, arms, legs and teeth as they were being carried through the door by the Alyeska guards.

At the end of the third run at the door the gunman shouted, "You'll never take me alive, copper!" which effectively destroyed the rest of Kate's gravity, and even Bernie turned away with his lips twitching. He tossed the trooper a damp towel and set up a round of drinks on the house. Everyone rushed for the bar, to knock theirs back and brag about how each of them had single-handedly disarmed the four, no, seven, wait, wasn't it twelve armed desperadoes who had taken a hundred people hostage in Bernie's Roadhouse on this memorable evening. Chopper Jim mopped off his uniform and accepted a ginger ale.

"This must be the most fun those rent-a-cops have had since Pump Eight blew up," Kate said to Jim Chopin.

"Hello, Kate," he said, still calm, hitching his gun belt up a notch over his hips, superbly unconcerned with the damp stains left on his uniform pants. "Haven't seen you this far inside the Park in a while."

"I'm looking for someone."

"I know."

She said involuntarily, "How the hell could you know?"

"I do come into contact with a few members of Alaska's law enforcement community from time to time." He grinned. Chopper Jim had a grin like a shark, wide, white and predatory, and knowing eyes that saw far too much. They had one effect on offenders of the law, and a completely different one on the opposite sex.

Kate stared at that grin and suddenly remembered she was of the opposite sex herself. "Er, of course," she said, giving herself a mental kick. I'm older than this, she reminded herself sternly.

Chopper Jim scratched Mutt's head with caressing fingers. She flattened her ears and wagged her tail slavishly. Make that the opposite sex of any species. "Found anything yet?" he said casually.

She hesitated. "Nothing for you to act on," she said

71

cautiously. "Some interesting coincidences."

"Want to share?"

She shook her head. "Not yet."

"If you need help—"

"Katya!" Kate looked around and was overrun by what at first glimpse seemed to be a smaller, pudgier and younger version of herself. "Katya, why didn't you tell me you were here? Why didn't you come find me?"

"I thought I had, Xenia," Kate said, chuckling at her cousin's overwhelming enthusiasm, and put a little on her guard as well. "Let's move to a table so we can talk. Nice seeing you, Jim."

Xenia looked up at the big trooper from beneath long lashes and blushed. "Hi, Jim."

The trooper touched the brim of his hat with two fingers. "Xenia."

Xenia tossed her hair over her shoulders and said, still looking at him from beneath her lashes, "You keep saying you'll come over to my house to visit the next time you're in Niniltna, Jim, but you never do. How come?"

The trooper looked her over from head to toe, slowly and carefully and thoroughly, the gaze of an experienced investigator trained to miss not the smallest detail. Sylvester looked at Tweety Bird that way. Hell, Kate thought, Atilla the Hun had looked at Rome that way. Xenia's blush became even rosier. "How old are you now, Xenia?" the trooper said.

"Not old enough," Kate said, pushing between them. "Good-bye, Jim." She took her cousin's elbow and steered her toward a vacant table on the other side of the room.

Xenia was dragging her feet, looking over her shoulder, and when Kate looked back Chopper Jim's teeth flashed again and he touched the brim of his hat. "Snap out of it, girl," Kate muttered to her cousin out of one corner of her mouth. "It's not for nothing they call Jim Chopin the Father of the Park."

They were barely seated before Xenia, her mood shifting mercurially, said in an urgent undertone, "Katya, could you get me a job in town?"

"I don't know," her cousin said, her eyes fixed on the girl's face. "What can you do?"

"Anything," Xenia said eagerly. "I can type, I can file, I got my high school diploma this year."

"Why this sudden urge to vacate the premises?"

"I want to get away," the younger girl said passionately. "I want to get out of this place. I want to go where there are cars and movies and restaurants and other kinds of people—"

"Like, maybe, men in uniform," Kate said, smiling a little.

Xenia colored and said defiantly, "Yes, anyone that isn't a dumb Native."

"Hold it now—"

"I don't care! If they aren't dumb, they're drunk, and if they're drunk they hurt people, they even—" She caught Kate's eyes and stopped suddenly. "I want to get away," she said in a plaintive voice.

The girl was young and fresh-faced and would have been pretty but for her sulky eyes and the petulant droop to her lower lip. "I don't know that just wanting to get away is the best reason for moving to town," Kate said slowly.

"You've seen emaa, haven't you?" Xenia said with quick suspicion. Kate nodded, and Xenia said with a bitterness that alarmed her cousin, "I knew it! I knew she'd get to you first and turn you against me and ruin my life! She wants me to stay here and learn how to weave baskets and carve ivory and spin qiviut and die of boredom! I hate her! I hate you!" Kate tried to say something and Xenia rushed on. "It's all so easy for you, you made it out, you went to school, you worked in town, you have a choice! Old Snow White, that's what we call you in the village! And now I'm stuck here in this—"

"Xenia!" Kate's voice was like the crack of a whip, and Xenia jumped and gulped back tears. "First of all, emaa didn't turn me against you. She talked to me, and yes, she wants me to convince you not to go to town." She held up one hand, palm out. "I didn't say I would."

Xenia's woeful face brightened at once. "Then you will help me! Oh, Katya, I knew I could count on you, I knew you would make everything right, when can I go?"

"Hold it! I didn't say I wouldn't try to talk you out of leaving, either." The girl opened her mouth to protest and Kate said sternly, "Let me finish, please." She stared the girl into sullen silence. "I want you to think about what you're doing, Xenia. I want you to think about what you'll be leaving behind. You think it's nothing. I tell you it can be everything. Here, you're surrounded by family and friends, good people you've known all your life, good people who know you, people you can turn to when you're in trouble, people who are always there for your birthday and Christmas and New Year's." Kate sat back in her chair and frowned at her folded hands. "It's different in Anchorage, Xenia. A lot different. In Anchorage you'd be on your own, and it can be very lonely in a big city after living in the bush."

"I don't care, I—"

"The kind of job you're qualified for doesn't pay much and you won't have a lot of money, and being in a city without money is like being hungry in the middle of a herd of caribou without a rifle."

"It doesn't matter, at least I—"

"You won't be able to buy a car until you save up," Kate

said inexorably. "And you'll probably have to share an apartment, which means you'll be thrown in at close quarters with someone you've never seen before in your life, maybe some Outsider who thinks Alaska Natives are as dumb as you do." Her raspy voice was cutting, and her cousin had the grace to look ashamed. "They'll make fun of you because you want to celebrate Christmas and New Year's in January the Russian Orthodox way. Others will resent you because you're a Native and you get something for what they think is nothing, ANCSA money and treatment at ANS just for being an Alaska Indian. Some of them will even ask you, and in front of other people, too, why you aren't down on Fourth Avenue with the rest of your relatives."

"I don't care, Katya," Xenia said in a small voice to the tabletop. "I just want out."

Kate searched her face for a long moment. "All right," she said at last. "Think over what I've said for a week or so. If you still feel the same way, I'll see what I can do."

"Oh, Katya, thank you! I knew you'd come through for me!"

"I haven't done anything yet," Kate said dryly. "In the meantime there is something you can do for me."

"What?"

"Emaa tells me you've been seeing one of the park rangers."

Prepared for a strong reaction, Kate was nevertheless shocked by the result of her question. The color drained out of Xenia's face, her body slackened and she swayed in her chair as if she were going to slide down to the sawdust-covered floor. Kate reached out quickly to steady her, but the girl waved her off with one shaking hand. "I'm all right," she muttered, avoiding her cousin's eyes.

"So you were seeing him," Kate said. "Mark Miller."

"Yes." The noise in the bar almost drowned out the girl's nearly inaudible response. She sat still as a parka squirrel scenting a fox.

Kate looked at her bent head, frowning. "Was it…serious?"

There was a brief silence. "I thought so," the girl said, seeming to pick her words with great care. "He said he loved me, that he was going to marry me and take me away from here."

"When was the last time you saw him?"

"Six weeks ago, October 26," the girl said promptly.

Kate raised an eyebrow. "You're very certain of the date."

"Yes." Still that almost inaudible voice.

"Did he tell you why he was leaving, where he was going?"

"He just left," Xenia said to the tabletop. "He didn't even leave me the key to his jeep."

"He left it here?"

"Sure," Xenia said, too carelessly. "Left it outside the Roadhouse to seize up in the cold. Dumb Outsider."

"Dumb," Kate said, her voice cool. "You use that word a lot. Dumb is anyone who doesn't do what you want them to, is that it?"

"No it's not!" Xenia's lip quivered. "Anyway, he left without saying a word. He lied to me and then he dumped me, okay? And if you don't mind I don't want to talk about it anymore. I'm going to get a ride back to town." The girl shoved back her chair and flounced out of the Roadhouse.

Kate sat looking thoughtfully after her cousin for a long time, and then rose and went to the bar. "Bernie?"

He came over. "Yeah?"

"Did you know Xenia was dating Mark Miller?"

Bernie reached for a glass and his bar rag and polished one with the other thoughtfully. "And if I did?"

Kate sighed. Bernie was that rarity, a bartender who didn't gossip about the private lives of his clientele. "If it was just Miller, Bernie, I'd write him off and tell the Park Service to go looking for the body when the snow melts. But the first person to come looking for Miller wound up missing, too, a guy named Ken Dahl. I brought him in here a couple of times."

"I remember. Blond guy, always shaking hands with somebody."

"That's the one," Kate said shortly. "Anyway, he came up here two weeks ago—"

"I know. He came in here, too." Bernie grinned. "Like I said, everybody comes to Bernie's."

Kate hid a long, silent intake of breath, and said, "Would you care to tell me about it?"

"About Miller or Dahl?"

"Let's start with Miller. He was seeing Xenia."

"Yup."

"Often?" Kate said patiently. It did no good to get irritable with Bernie; he'd just close up like a clam and invite you out of his bar. He had a sign hung over the back of his bar which read, we reserve the right to refuse service, and Bernie took that to be his credo, his guiding light, his raison d'être, right up there next to no customers allowed behind the bar and free throws win ball games. "Bernie?" Kate repeated when he didn't reply.

Bernie inspected the polished glass critically. "I'd call every night often."

Kate raised her eyebrows. "So would I. How serious do you think it was?"

Bernie gave up on the glass and started wiping the bar rag back and forth across the bar in long, ruminative strokes. "He was damn serious. Of course, I don't know that he liked her as much as he liked the fact that she was part of the Park." He smiled a little. "She was indigenous to the place, like the copper and the caribou. He did tell me one night he was planning on marrying her and living here happy ever after."

"She told me he promised to take her out of here," Kate said.

Bernie shrugged. "Xenia always did think she could make the three-pointer when an assist on a lay-up was all that was in the playbook." The bar rag stilled, and Bernie raised calm brown eyes, as if to examine the effect his next words would produce. "Martin didn't like it."

Kate stared at him. "Xenia's brother?" she said. "He didn't like her going out with Miller?"

"No," Bernie said judiciously, "actually that's not quite true. Martin hated it. He hated Xenia going out with an Anglo and an Outsider in the first place, and then he found out Miller was a ranger. Talk about adding insult to injury. He got pretty loud about it."

Kate felt a sense of foreboding. "Where did he get pretty loud about it?"

Bernie nodded toward the room at large. "Right here. That last night anyone saw Miller, Martin walked in about one o'clock that morning and caught him and Xenia dancing and smooching it up. They had words. The damages cost Martin a hundred bucks, which is about par for him."

"You mean they had a fight?"

"I don't care what anybody says about you, Kate," Bernie said admiringly, "you are smarter than the average bear. It was the day of that hearing on building a road into the Park. Everybody came down to the Roadhouse for a drink after the committee adjourned, and stayed on. There were about fifty witnesses. Most of them took bets on the fight, and helped pick up the tables and chairs afterward."

"And then Miller disappears off the face of the earth," Kate muttered. "Wonderful."

"I'd say that about summed up the situation," Bernie agreed.

Kate thought about it for a while. "Xenia says Miller left his jeep here the night he disappeared."

"Sure. It's still sitting out back." He grinned. "What's left of it. I'll show you."

She shrugged into her snowsuit and followed him outside, Mutt trotting behind her. It was perceptibly colder than when she had come in, and her breath made puffs of vapor that hung behind her in the air. She pulled her hood up around her face.

The Jeep was a Toyota Land Cruiser—because of its high ground clearance, small turning radius and four-wheel drive, one of the most popular vehicles in the Park—which explained why Miller's vehicle was now missing all four tires and wheels, as well as the spare, the battery, the plugs, the filter, the distributor cap, one of the bucket seats, the windshield and the driver's side door. There was a pile of dog turds, frozen hard, between the front and back seats, and one of those air fresheners in the shape of an evergreen hanging from the rearview mirror, and that was all.

"There isn't a lot left to it, is there?" Kate observed.

"Not much sense in letting it sit here, freezing up into a piece of junk," Bernie said cheerfully.

"No," Kate admitted.

Along with the missing parts there was not the vestige of a clue to be found beneath the remaining seats or in the glove compartment or the wheel wells or in any one of half a dozen other places Kate thought to look.

"So, Sherlock," Bernie said. Standing in his T-shirt and jeans and thongs, he made Kate shiver just to look at him. "What next?"

"Did Miller say anything that last evening that would indicate what he was going to do next, where he was going after he left the Roadhouse?"

Bernie shook his head. "He was just a little guy, Kate, and you know Martin. Miller looked like he was having a hard time keeping up off all fours. I figured he was heading home to bed."

"Where was Xenia?"

"She'd run out of the bar during the fight." Bernie's voice did not change. "She never was much good on defense."

Kate was silent, and Bernie said, "Wait a minute. Early on Miller did say something about trying to make a call, and goddaming NorthCom. He didn't say when, or who to, so that don't really mean nothing."

Kate hunched further down into her snowsuit. "Did you tell Ken Dahl all this?"

"Some of it," Bernie said. "Not all."

"Why not?"

Bernie shrugged and started back in. "He said he was an investigator. I figured, let him investigate." He paused and looked back at her. "Funny thing about this jeep."

"Funny ha-ha or funny strange?"

"Funny strange. I left the bar around two-thirty that morning to go over to the house and grab a sandwich. This jeep wasn't here then."

Kate stared at Bernie. "You're sure?"

Bernie nodded.

"When did you see it next?"

"I sleep in mornings. The jeep was right here when I come

over to open up the bar at twelve o'clock that afternoon." He grinned. "I remember because Abel was waiting for me to pour out his weekly bourbon."

She gave an involuntary smile. "He still comes in every week?"

"Like clockwork."

"Just the one shot?"

"Just the one."

She chuckled, but her amusement soon faded and she said, without much hope, "Enid didn't happen to see anything?"

He shook his head. "Or the kids neither."

Kate stood still, thinking. "So he went somewhere, and then he came back."

"It looks that way."

"But when? And then where did he go from here?"

Bernie shrugged. "That I couldn't tell you. There's so much traffic around here nights, I wouldn't know exactly when any one truck or snow machine or dogsled came or left." He grinned. "A D-9 Cat, of course, is pretty hard to miss."

"Or a helicopter," she said, and they both laughed. Her laughter faded and, frowning, she said, "And why would he come back? To pick up Xenia, maybe?"

Bernie shook his head. "Xenia ducked out early in the fight. I didn't see her again that night."

Kate sighed. "I better get on over to NorthCom, then. Maybe Miller got a call and had to leave on a family emergency, or something like that."

Bernie looked at her.

"Oh shut up," Kate said, and climbed on her Super Jag for the trip back to the village.

CHAPTER 5

THE NORTHCOM SHACK WAS located within the city limits, fifty feet up the road from the Niniltna School. The shack was just that, a one-room shack made of plywood stapled to two-by-four uprights, crowned with asphalt shingles, lined between its two-by-fours with the ubiquitous pink Owens Corning insulation found beneath every Sheetrock wall in the state. The Andrews five-meter dish stood on its own tower out back, tilted on its polar mount true north 61 degrees from the horizontal to track Northern Light, the state's personal communications satellite.

There wasn't any line outside the door, an unusual sight that filled Kate with a sense of quiet satisfaction. Before the state legislature in 1986 passed a law that permitted local communities to ban alcohol, Niniltna's NorthCom earth station accounted for some $800,000 a year in money orders, ninety-five percent of which were booze orders to liquor stores in Anchorage. Since the tribal council had passed what Park locals referred to as the DampAct, and sometimes the GodDampAct, revenues had fallen to less than a fourth of what they had been. Local air taxi services had seen a boom in charter flights to the nearest liquor store, a hundred and thirty miles away. There were rumors NorthCom was thinking of shutting the Niniltna earth station down entirely, which would leave Niniltna and everyone else in the Park dependent for communications on the two ham operators operating within the confines of the Park, the shortwave between Anchorage and the Park monitored by Chugach Air Taxi Service, and the weekly mail flown into Niniltna each Monday, weather permitting, also courtesy Chugach Air.

There was no one inside. Usually the operator, who with an alternate worked a month on and a month off, slept on a cot in the back. A shelf held his hot plate and tiny refrigerator, and it was all screened by a curtain of faded cotton with a blue floral pattern and kept warm by an Earth stove. The local wood seller figured the operator must have come from somewhere Outside originally, down south and way down, because he burned at least a cord of wood in that Earth stove every month.

Kate banged the bell on the counter. Mutt stood a step behind her, trying to look as if she didn't know perfectly well that she was supposed to wait outside.

"All right, all right," came a voice from behind the curtain. "Hold your horses, I'm coming."

There were some whispers and a few giggles before the operator appeared around the edge of the flowered curtain, clad in mismatched wool socks that left far too much of his thin, hairy legs exposed, jockey shorts and a flannel shirt he was still buttoning. His lank brown hair was all over the place and his face looked very pleased with itself and invited Kate to be, too. He stretched and yawned and scratched. "What can I do you for?"

"Sorry to bother you," Kate said, hiding a grin. "I'm looking for information about a park ranger named Mark Miller."

There was a gasp and a sudden immobility from behind the curtain. Kate's inner grin faded. She stepped swiftly around the counter, shoved the operator out of the way and swept back the curtain to reveal Xenia cowering on the cot, naked beneath the grubby sheet clutched to her chin. She met Kate's eyes defiantly.

Kate let the curtain fall and went back around the counter and looked at the operator. "Do you know who Mark Miller is?"

The operator, fully awake now, eyed her warily and gave a cautious nod. "Park ranger, new one." His eyes slid to the curtain and then back. "He's missing."

"Yes. I'm looking for him."

"Who for?"

"Does it matter?"

The operator's eyes slid to the curtain again. He said nothing.

"Can you remember the last time he was in here?"

"The privacy of any communication through the public communications system of the state of Alaska is protected by both state and federal law," he recited.

"And by the Bill of Rights and the Constitution of the United States and probably by d-2, too," Kate agreed. "So what? I haven't asked you to divulge the contents of any outgoing messages. I just want to know if he sent one."

He said nothing. Kate snapped her fingers in front of his eyes, and he transferred his gaze from the curtain to her face. "What's your name?"

"Melvin Haney."

"How long have you had this job?"

"Four months."

"Uh-huh." Kate folded her arms on the counter and leaned forward. "Melvin, my name is Kate Shugak." His eyes widened, and dropped involuntarily to her throat, hidden by the

84

turtleneck of her long underwear. "Mark Miller is the son of a United States congressman, and this congressman has set the FBI on his boy's trail." Melvin's eyes widened further, and at last Kate felt she had his complete attention. "The FBI went to the Anchorage District Attorney for help in locating the young man, and the Anchorage District Attorney came to me."

Kate smiled kindly at the young man, showing all her teeth. He flinched perceptibly. "Now, Melvin, I'm telling you all this so you'll know that law enforcement at every level in this country is interested in your answers to my questions here tonight. If I don't like them, your answers, that is, then the District Attorney's office won't like them, and if the D.A. doesn't like them, the feds won't like them, and if the feds don't like them, the congressman sure as hell isn't going to like them, either. When that happens, I won't have any trouble getting the Niniltna Native Association to request the Alaska Beverage Commission and maybe even the Bureau of Alcohol, Tobacco and Firearms to make a trip up here to sift through your back invoices for the last six months, just to assure themselves that you've been abiding by the DampAct." Kate gave him another wide smile. Mutt suddenly reared up to place both paws on the counter, and she showed all her teeth, too, in a display of concern over the tension she heard in Kate's voice.

He hesitated. "You Xenia's cousin? That Kate Shugak?"

Kate kept her smile fixed to her face and pitched her torn voice to carry. "I can't say I'm flattered by any resemblance you might imagine you see. Talk to me. When was the last time you saw Mark Miller?"

He regarded the two sets of glistening canines gleaming at him from not far enough away and capitulated. "The night he disappeared."

"You're that sure about the date?"

He nodded. "I would have remembered anyway because he made such a fuss about getting a call through. Couldn't do it because the dish was down. He wasn't the first one to come in here and rant; I had outgoing stuff backed up for twenty-four hours."

Frowning, Kate said, "What did you mean, you would have remembered anyway?"

He shrugged. "There was another guy looking for him about two weeks ago. He pinned me down on the day Miller was in."

"Blond, blue-eyed?" she asked.

"Talked like Teddy Kennedy running for office?"

"Jesus Christ," Kate said under her breath. "Yeah, that's him. He say where he was going after he talked to you?"

"The ranger or the blond?"

"The blond."

"No."

"How about the ranger, he say where he was going?"

"Nope." Again his eyes slid to the curtain and back to her. "But everybody knows he went out to the Roadhouse. His car's out there."

She nodded. "Did you see him in it? Did you see him actually driving the Toyota?"

"Yeah."

Kate looked at him and said, "What do you think happened to him?"

"Beats me." He looked again at the curtain. "First I heard he was gone was when O'Brian over to Park Headquarters sent the message to Washington, D.C."

Kate nodded again. "Did you like him? Miller, I mean."

He looked confused. "I didn't hardly know him."

Kate looked deliberately at the curtain, and back to him. "Anything else you can remember?"

Awareness came slowly, and when it did his eyes popped and he shook his head violently. "I told you, I didn't hardly know the guy at all."

"Uh-huh," Kate said in a neutral voice.

He swallowed and said, "You think he's dead?"

She looked behind him at the curtain and raised her voice one more time. "That, or he left because he knows there's nothing to hold him here." She looked back at the NorthCom operator and said with another smile, "Or he was removed because he was in the way."

She closed the door behind her and heard the operator say plaintively through the thin door, "And what the hell is that when it's at home?" She heard Xenia mumble a reply, and moved out to the porch.

Pulling the door to behind her, she stood on the doorstep for a long time, breathing the cold air deep into her chest. She was ashamed of herself, using that boy as a target to get to Xenia. They were just a couple of kids doing what came naturally on cold winter nights in Niniltna. The kid had showed some backbone, too, and Kate liked that.

Still. Every instinct she possessed told her that Xenia knew something she wasn't telling her cousin. She wondered how long it would take to get it out of her. She never doubted for a moment that she would, but in spite of her fierce rejection of family responsibility, her protective instincts where the younger members of her family were involved ran strong and deep. They would not permit her the luxury of an all-out frontal assault. But a little gentle prodding and Xenia would remember all the times good old cousin Kate had kept Tiny Mike the school bully from beating up on her. Eventually she would decide that Kate was after all a fit person to confide in. She made plans to return to her grandmother's house early the next morning.

The light from the uncurtained window in the shack's door streamed out into the arctic night, clearly outlining her figure on the top step. She heard a snap like ice cracking on a frozen lake, a whine like a super-charged hornet past her cheek and a *splat* as the bullet carved a furrow into the door and lodged in the jamb.

Mutt barked once, a sharp, warning sound. Kate took a giant leap and hurled herself down the short, steep flight of stairs and behind the berm of snow that lined the path to the shack. Her shoulder hit first and she rolled into a crouch, her heart pounding so loudly that for a few moments she could hear nothing else. Her body felt instantaneously cold all over, right down into each individual digit. She felt as if she had X-ray eyes, that she could hear and decipher with bare ear the signals coming in via the satellite dish behind her, that she was able to smell the decay of summer grass buried deep beneath hard-packed snow. Every one of her senses was receiving such an overload of information that she was too busy collating it all to be scared. She had never felt more alive in her life.

"What the hell was that?" she heard the NorthCom operator yell. She heard the smack of bare feet as Xenia hit the floor, and knew her cousin would be fleeing in a panic out the door in moments.

"Stay where you are!" she yelled, or tried to. Her maimed throat made it difficult. She eeled herself backward, beneath the steps, and spoke as loudly as she could through the floor. Mutt, clearly puzzled, slunk along beside her, her ears up in inquiry, whining a little. "Stay where you are," she repeated.

"It's some nut with a gun up at the school. Get down behind the counter and stay there."

She kicked the floor for emphasis. "Stay!" she told Mutt, and slid back over the hard-packed snow. She risked a look up over the berm. Nothing. She stretched out flat and slithered on her belly down the icy path to where the walkway met Niniltna's main street. A quick peek from behind the snow piled at the side of the street revealed no stir of movement. She got up on all fours and picked her way over dog turds and Snickers wrappers and empty plastic Windsor Canadian whiskey bottles, carefully keeping her head below the level of the snow berm. When the berm ended in the school's parking lot she paused, stiffened her spine and risked another look up over it.

There was a second crack and a splatter of snow over her face. At the same time a heavy weight hit her in the small of the back, laying her out flat on her stomach. Mutt growled out a bark and she heard a scrabble of padded feet.

The breath had been knocked out of her, and all she could do for the next few moments was lie there trying to get it back. She waited for Mutt to tear the head off of whoever was on top of her.

The dog skidded to a halt less than three feet away; Kate could see her clearly from where her cheek was pressed against the cold snow. Mutt growled once, barked once and then flattened her ears and wagged her tail.

"You all right, girl?" a voice rasped in her ear.

Kate got her breath back with a rush. "Abel?"

"Who else?"

"Get off me, you old fart!"

Abel slid to the snow next to her and jacked a round into the bolt-action Winchester Model 54 that was almost as old as he was and that he always carried with him just in case he met up with a bull moose in rut or a Fish and Game agent, whichever came first. He pulled his legs up under him, popped up behind the berm and let off a round in the general direction of the school. "Just to let the bastard know we got teeth, too," he said reassuringly as he flopped back down next to her. "Who's shooting at you?"

"I don't know."

"Hmm." Abel worked the bolt of his rifle and pulled himself upright again.

"Abel, no!"

This time the shooter was waiting. As soon as Abel's torso cleared the berm there was a shot. Abel returned fire and fell back down next to Kate with a thump.

"Goddam you, old man!"

Abel's eyes were screwed shut as he groped around near his right shoulder. One eye opened and surveyed her with disfavor. "You're beginning to repeat yourself, girl."

Kate crouched over him and yanked his hand down from his shoulder. With it came a handful of down pulled out of the torn sleeve of his parka, a cloud of tiny feathers which caught in her hair and flew into her eyes and were inhaled up her nose. She sneezed once, violently, and glared at him. There was no wound, no blood. She felt a wave of relief supersede the roil of terror, and glared all the harder. "And I'll keep repeating myself until you hear me, old man. You keep getting in my way, goddammit. I won't have it, do you hear?"

His head came up off the snow. "Yeah."

"Yeah what?"

"Yeah, I hear that bugger who was just shooting at us beating feet outa here."

Kate became aware of pounding footsteps moving away

from the back of the school gym. A swell of pure rage heaved her to her feet in one surging movement. "Mutt! *Fetch!*"

Mutt hit the ground running, a gray streak stretched out low, skimming over the snow like a ghost. Even as she vanished around the dark bulk of the gymnasium, they heard a snow machine splutter into life and roar off. Kate cursed and ran after the dog.

The lot was empty of anything but snow and ice and what looked like one of Dandy Mike's half-breed husky—German shepherds who, seeing her, came trotting over to sniff interestedly at her crotch. Mutt, looking for a fight in her frustration at not catching whoever had had the audacity to shoot at her very own private human, growled a loud and toothy warning.

"It's all right, Mutt," Kate said, beating back her rage and fear. She knew just how Mutt felt. She slapped the other dog's nose away and began a search of the area, doubled over with her nose nearly touching the snow. It was too late; whoever it was had disappeared into the night. And they'd either picked up their shell casings or she couldn't find them in the dark. The old snow, worn down by a healthy and energetic student body, grades one through twelve, was not the best surface on which to find tracks. It was so dry and hard it squeaked underfoot. Kate gave it up in disgust and walked back to the road.

"Guess we scared the bugger off," Abel observed complacently.

Kate shook her head. "Abel, Abel, Abel," she said, still shaking her head and trying to keep her knees from doing the same. "What am I going to do with you? You could have been shot. You could have been killed."

"Well, I wasn't," he said testily, "and it seems to me we

91

should stir around and find out who that bugger was instead of standing here freezing to death, moaning over whether or not I should be here!"

"What are you doing here, anyway?" Kate said.

No answer. Abel bent over to retrieve his moose exterminator and occupied himself with removing every speck of snow or ice that might or might not have found its way into the mechanism.

Kate, half-amused, half-exasperated, said, "You think I can't take care of myself, is that it? You raised me to, Abel."

"I ain't saying a word." Abel's jaw set stubbornly. "All I know is a guy's missing, and the guy that went after him went missing, too, and if it's cold now it'll be twice that when I have to come looking for you when you go missing. You and your goddam loaded pipeliners."

Kate's eyes widened. "Abel, were you at the Roadhouse this evening?" she demanded.

"I ain't saying a word." He sighted carefully along the barrel of his rifle. "Maybe I was and maybe I wasn't. Somebody had to put in a call to make sure Chopper Jim was on his way."

Kate, wanting to order him home, knowing he wouldn't go, praying he wouldn't get in the way, knowing he would, gave it up and resigned herself to a second guard dog. "Well, all I know is it's a little late now to decide you were a lousy teacher."

"I ain't saying a word," he said, shedding a glove to pick at a minute speck of ice on the Winchester's trigger guard.

"Fine," she said, and stamped back to the NorthCom shack, where she found the NorthCom operator and Xenia shivering in the doorway. Xenia jumped the three steps in a single leap and clutched at Kate. "Did you see who it was, Katya? Did you catch him?"

"No."

Xenia's grip relaxed and her hands slid down to her sides.

Kate looked thoughtfully at her cousin's tense, frightened face. "You and I are going to have ourselves a little talk, Xenia." She looked from her cousin to the NorthCom operator. "Mind if we use your place?"

"Sure, I—" The kid caught her eye and cleared his throat. "Uh, yeah. I was just about to go down to the store to, uh, buy some milk, anyway."

Xenia said, "But the store closes at six."

He gestured vaguely. "Well, then, I'll go borrow a cup from Mickey Komkoff. Back in a flash." He disappeared into the shack and reappeared attired in pants, parka and boots. He gave Xenia a loud, smacking kiss, Kate a pointed look daring her to object, and headed up the path.

Kate pushed her reluctant cousin into the shack and closed the door on Abel's bright, inquisitive gaze. Xenia went to the room's only chair and sat down, folding her arms tightly across her chest.

"I want the truth this time, Xenia," Kate said sternly. "All of it."

The girl was silent, hugging herself.

"What do you think happened to Mark Miller that you're not telling me?" Xenia said nothing. Kate, suddenly furious with the selfish little brat, strode across to where she was sitting and hauled her up out of her chair by the front of her shirt. "He said he loved you, Xenia, and he's missing and he might be dead, and now someone's shooting at me probably because they don't want me to find out. Don't you care? If not about Miller, then about me?" She snarled out the last words.

Xenia looked at her out of brown eyes bright with tears. She looked about six years old. Kate loosened her grip on

Xenia's shirt, and the girl slid out of her grasp and onto the floor as if her legs were made of warm wax. She pulled her knees up and hid her face in them and spoke without looking at Kate. "You'll find me a job in Anchorage? You promise? You'll get me away from here?"

Kate unzipped her snowsuit and peeled it down to her waist. She sat down next to her cousin and tried to temper the disgust and exasperation she felt. "I'd do that anyway. From what I've seen in the last eight hours, the sooner you get out of Niniltna the better. No, no, never mind that now. Just tell me what happened the night Mark Miller disappeared."

What happened the night of October 26 was that Xenia and Mark Miller had made a date to meet at Bernie's Roadhouse, since Ekaterina had made it clear the ranger wasn't welcome in Ekaterina's house, Xenia's home since her mother and father had died in a plane crash three years before. "Then Martin came in," Xenia said, tears in her brown eyes, "and caught us dancing together. He grabbed Mark and hit him, and Mark hit him back, and pretty soon the whole bar was fighting." The tearful brown gaze fell back to her knees. "I was scared, so I ran."

"You left the Roadhouse?"

"Yes."

"You left Mark behind?"

"I told you I was scared, and he's a man, he could take care of himself."

"An Outsider, a greenie, against a bar full of Moonins and Shugaks?"

The girl gave a petulant shrug. "What about me? I had to walk home all alone, from the Roadhouse back to town, in the cold. You know what happens to people who do that." She gasped and bit her lip, looking at Kate with frightened eyes.

"Yes, I know," Kate said without emotion. "What happened next?"

"Like I said, I started walking home. I was almost to the Lost Chance Creek bridge before I heard a car. I turned around to wave and I saw that it was Martin's pickup and so I ducked down next to the bridge railing and waited for it to go over the bridge. But it didn't."

"What did it do?" The girl's shoulders shook, and Kate repeated implacably, "What did the truck do?"

"It stopped in the middle of the bridge and two men got out and started messing around with something in the back. It was dark and I couldn't see very well and besides I was—"

"You were scared," Kate said.

The girl gave her a resentful look and said sullenly, "Well, I was."

"So you were scared," Kate said impatiently. "So would I have been, so would anyone. I'm not judging you." At least I'm trying like hell not to, she thought. "What happened next?"

"So I ducked down and waited. The guys were grunting and staggering like whatever was in the back was heavy. I heard footsteps go from the pickup to the side of the bridge, and then I heard the splash." She started to cry again. "Martin'll kill me if he knows I told you. I've got to get out of here, Katya!"

"You're sure it was Martin's truck?" Kate said relentlessly, ignoring the tears.

Xenia gulped back a sob. "Yes. I saw the license plate and that dented tailgate he got when the fish hawk ran him off the road to serve that warrant, you know, for that time Martin got caught seining behind the markers on Teglliq Creek. Martin always said those markers were too far out—"

"Never mind the fish hawk and the Teglliq Creek markers. Did you see who the second man was?"

"No, I told you, I was too scared to look, and they didn't talk much, except to swear."

Kate was silent for a long time. At last she stirred and stood up. "All right, Xenia."

"Are you going to talk to Martin?"

Kate looked at her with narrowed eyes. "Of course I am."

"Are you going to tell him I told you?" Xenia trembled and began to cry again. "You can't tell him, you can't, he'll kill me!"

"Don't whine, for God's sake," Kate snapped. "If he didn't see you and you haven't told him you were there, all I have to tell him is that there was a witness. He doesn't have to know who."

"And you'll get me that job in Anchorage, Katya? And maybe a place to stay?"

"Shut up, Xenia," Kate said from between clenched teeth. "Just shut up."

"Oh, it's always been so easy for you," the girl cried, "old Snow White! You never do anything wrong and you're never afraid! Katya! Where are you going?" she said, the tears beginning to flow a third time.

"Bobby's." Kate turned, and added over her shoulder, "If anyone asks for me and they're carrying a rifle, try not to tell them where I am, okay?"

CHAPTER 6

HE HAD HIS HEADPHONES on, lost in a wide-band frequency fog, and didn't answer when Kate knocked, so she opened the door that was always unlocked and went in and tapped him on the shoulder.

He jumped about a foot off his chair and slewed around to glare at her. Recognition came at once. "Goddam, woman," he roared, ripping his headphones off and slamming them down, "I told you a million times not to sneak up on me like that!"

Mutt jumped up to rest her forepaws on his shoulders and swiped at his face with a long pink tongue. "Goddam, woman," Bobby roared again, fending her off, "you got that fucking wolf with you! I told you before, no fucking wolves in the house!"

Unintimidated, Mutt swiped at him again and, formal greetings duly exchanged, got down and trotted over to the fireplace to root purposefully through the wood box, eventually producing something roughly on the scale of the femur of a stegosaurus. Bobby, a forward thinker, always had something in the wood box to keep the wolves at bay. Mutt settled down in the front of the fireplace and began to gnaw with an expression of almost sinful content.

Kate wiped Bobby's scowling face and leaned forward to kiss him. The roar shut off and he leaned into the kiss with enthusiasm. He opened one eye in the middle of the kiss to make sure she was enjoying it as much as he was and saw Abel standing in the open doorway regarding them with deep disapproval and a terrifying scowl.

"Oh," Bobby said, freeing his lips but not noticeably terrified and not releasing Kate. "Hello, Abel."

"Bobby," Abel said, nodding. "I got you here safe, girl. I'm heading over to Ekaterina's now. I'll be back in the morning."

"You're welcome to stay here, Abel," Bobby said. He let one enormous paw settle on Kate's left hip.

The old man bent his head stiffly. "'Preciate it, Bobby, but it's been a bit since I stirred up the old broad. I'm looking forward to it." He looked around Bobby's cabin with raised brows. "And she's always got a room"—he emphasized the word pointedly—"for me."

"Abel?" Kate said, twisting in Bobby's hands to look at him. "Thanks."

Abel bent his head again, and left.

Bobby watched the door close behind him. "Don't mind him, Bobby," she said in a low voice. "He's just old."

"I don't," he said, and then, surprisingly, "He reminds me of my old man. He wouldn't approve of this either." Bobby grinned lecherously and kissed Kate again, and then a sneaky third time before she could wriggle free.

"Who are you talking to tonight?" she said, breathless, tugging away from him with difficulty and indicating the radio.

"King Hussein of Jordan," he said. She laughed, and he raised his eyebrows and said, "You want to say hello?"

Diverted, she said, "Really? Hussein's a ham?"

"Virginia smoked, like myself," he said. "Want to talk to him?"

"I'd rather talk to Viktor."

"Ah, that sumbitchin' spy must have got himself arrested in the latest coup; he ain't been on the air for six months now. Want some coffee?"

"Sure."

He scratched his head and said, "Now that I come to think of it, I haven't had my supper. How about some food?"

She smiled wanly. "Come to think of it, I haven't had my supper either."

"What sounds good?"

"Everything," she said fervently.

"Lemme seventy-three His Majesty and I'll get right on it." He spoke into his mike, holding one side of the headphones to one ear, and switched his set off.

Kate watched him. He had the typical bulk of the wheelchair jockey, thick through the shoulders, chest and arms. Coal black from head to thigh, skin, eyes and hair, tonight he was dressed in black as well, jeans, shirt, even the T-shirt showing beneath his collar. "Why do I get the feeling that if you had feet you'd be wearing black socks and shoes, too?" Kate said as he hung up his headphones.

"Color coordination is everything," he said, smoothing his tight black curls complacently.

"Uh-huh," she said.

"Also makes me easier to spot from the air if I get lost in a daytime blizzard," he told her and grinned the friendly, infectious grin that could blind you if you weren't careful.

The wheels of his chair squeaked on the polished hardwood floor. There were no carpets in Bobby's house, unusual even in the poorest Alaskan home. No real Alaskan liked putting his or her bare feet on a barer floor on cold winter mornings. Bobby didn't care, mainly because he had no feet, having lost both legs up to and including the knee in Vietnam during the Tet Offensive. Ten years later he materialized in the Park, six months before Jimmy Carter created seventeen new national parks out of fifty-six million Alaskan acres, and therefore just in time to stake a claim on Squaw Candy Creek, a tributary of the Kanuyaq two miles upstream of Niniltna.

Kate never learned what he had been doing during the intervening decade, but since he had enough money to import lumber and a water pump and an electric generator and a thousand-gallon fuel tank from Anchorage, and hire labor from the town to construct his homestead, and had shown nary a sign of starving since, she had her own suspicions. He was the National Oceanic and Atmospheric Association's weather observer inside the Park, monitoring all the tedious statistics of temperature and wind speed and wind chill and humidity and precipitation and barometric pressure, and making the delicate daily differentiation between cumulus, altocumulus and fracto-cumulus every six hours. The pittance received for this sedentary and very boring job was enough to keep Bobby in controlled recreational substances that came twelve fifths to a case with "Product of Kentucky" stamped on the outside, but the rest of the time he seemed to subsist, and subsist well, on barter and air.

Bobby wheeled his chair around on the bare wood floor, popped a wheelie just to remind Kate he could, and scooted over to the kitchen. Bobby liked speed in non-chemical form, on his snow machine, in his specially modified, souped-up Cessna 170 and in his two customized wheelchairs around the house.

"Two?" Kate had commented the first time she saw the second one. "Why two?"

"Well, it's this way, Kate," he'd said expansively, wheeling around her in a tight circle to show off his precision cornering. "This one's for when I feel like chasing something." He sent her a friendly leer, and she laughed. "Like today. The other one has a motor."

"For when you don't feel frisky," she'd suggested.

"Or for when I have a hangover," he added, clarifying things.

Bobby's house was one big, square room without any inner walls or doors except to the bathroom. The center of the room was taken up by a four-sided work area crammed with electronic equipment and books, with multiple cables leading up the center pillar and through the roof to a forest of antennae and instrumentation and wiring that in daylight looked as if it were ready to lift into orbit. There was a teak shelf running the length of one wall, filled with record albums in their original jackets and almost in their original state at sale. No one handled them except Bobby, and he took them out only to record them on new cassettes after the old cassettes wore out. He was waiting for DAT to come out, at which time he intended to convert to CDs, but in the meantime he defiantly maintained his record collection and made life for the clerks at Robber Joe's Records in Anchorage a living hell tracking down out-of-print albums. Kate had placed some of his orders there, and the expressions on their faces when they saw her coming always made her feel a little sorry for them.

An enormous bed was shoved up against one wall, a couch and couple of easy chairs against another, with an open rock fireplace between them. In the kitchen the sink, the stove top and the counters didn't quite come up to Kate's hips but were perfect for Bobby to reach from his chair. There were windows from floor to ceiling on the wall that faced south. Through those windows, the full moon cast a serene glow over the ice-encrusted spruce, outlining the Quilaks' snow-crowned peaks to the east and teasing at the thin current of water running swiftly between the frozen shores of Squaw Candy Creek.

Kate built up the fire, which while meeting his radio schedule Bobby had as usual forgotten to feed, so that the inside of the house was almost as cold as the outside. The flames caught and crackled, and she subsided on the couch with a grunt of relief. The tension coiled in her belly began to ease.

"So what brings you into Niniltna, Katie?" he asked, zipping across the room with a steaming mug balanced on one arm of his chair. Before she could answer or thank him he zipped back to the kitchen to load up with a grill, ground caribou patties, buns and the rest of the makings.

"Don't forget the mustard," she said, and he opened a cupboard and added another jar to the tray on his lap. French's, she saw. Bobby spared no expense. He whizzed back across the hardwood floor to the fireplace and unburdened himself on the raised hearth. He raked some coals to the front of the fireplace, set up the grill and slapped down the meat.

It started sizzling immediately. Kate's mouth watered. She hadn't had anything to eat since Ekaterina's fried bread that afternoon. "Jack Morgan came to see me yesterday. He wants me to find someone for him."

"Who?" Bobby said without turning around.

"A park ranger, name of Mark Miller. You meet him?"

"Yeah."

"Seen him lately?"

Bobby shrugged. "Don't pal around with him enough to have kept track. Little guy, right? About as relaxed as Alexander Haig? Heard he was sweet on Xenia."

"Uh-huh," Kate said. "Can't you hurry those burgers up?"

"You want to cook?"

"No," Kate said immediately, "no, I'm sorry, Bobby, I won't kibitz any more, I promise." She held her breath.

"See you don't," Bobby sniffed. "How long's this Miller been missing?"

Kate relaxed. She would eat after all. "Six weeks."

"Hmm. I suppose the usual explanation won't do?"

Kate shook her head, and then, remembering Bobby couldn't see her, said out loud, "Nope."

"Why not?"

"Because Jack sent someone in to look for him, and now he's missing, too."

There was a hiss of sizzling fat as Bobby pressed the spatula against the burgers. "What's the Anchorage District Attorney doing looking for a missing federal employee? I thought the feds had people who do that for them."

"Enter the FBI."

Bobby turned to look at her, a long, hard, black stare. "Just who the hell is this park ranger related to, anyway?"

Kate smiled faintly. "A U.S. congressman."

Bobby, still staring, took it in, thought it over and nodded as if all his worst suspicions had been confirmed. "They go to Jack for help?"

"Yeah."

"And he came to you."

"Yeah. I feel like I've told this story a hundred times since this morning."

"Who've you been talking to?"

She ticked them off on her fingers. "Abel, Mandy, Emaa, Bernie, Xenia, the new NorthCom operator—come to think of it, what happened to the old NorthCom operator?"

He shot her a broad, over-the-shoulder grin. "The tribal

council—how did Billy Mike put it?—" Bobby deepened his voice and rolled the words off his tongue with all the authority of a Shakespearean actor. "'...brought pressure to bear on Taylor Benson's employer, one Far North Communications Corporation, and recommended that although no proof had been found to implicate Taylor Benson in the nefarious deeds of one Harold C. "Sandy" Halvorsen, Park bootlegger emeritus, that said Taylor Benson had nevertheless proved less than vigilant in overseeing and alerting the council to the unusual number of orders for antifreeze placed by the same Mr. Halvorsen, and the tribal council would be grateful if he was removed from his post forthwith.'"

"Billy Mike didn't say all that."

"Did too!"

"He didn't use the word 'nefarious,' I know that much for a fact." Kate added, "Or 'forthwith,' either."

Bobby shrugged and she heard the laugh in his voice. "I may have—er—prettied it up a little. For the sake of the story."

"You have been known to do that," Kate agreed, deadpan.

"It is, however," Bobby said, "absolutely true that in a three-month period Halvorsen ordered enough Shell antifreeze from town to winterize the *Nimitz*, and that Taylor never turned a hair. But you know all that." Kate nodded without replying, and Bobby looked at her curiously. "Billy Mike says that when he first asked you to do something about Sandy's operation, you told him you weren't a maid and to clean up his own house. What changed your mind?"

She gave a short bark of mirthless laughter. "Not what, who. Bernie."

"What about him?"

"He rode out to see me the day after I sent Billy on his way." Kate leaned back and smiled tiredly at the ceiling. "It wasn't the competition he minded so much, he told me. But Sandy was using kids out of junior high as rumrunners, and they were missing basketball practice."

Bobby laughed in spite of himself, and Kate grinned and said, "Yeah. And then there was Abel."

"Who was just itching for a chance to back you up."

There was a tinge of bitterness in Bobby's voice, and Kate changed the subject. "That new NorthCom kid, he sure is—" She hesitated. "He sure is new, isn't he?"

Bobby craned his neck to grin at her. "I heard that. We had him eating fish head stew last time we was all down to the Roadhouse together. You should have seen him when the eyes rolled up to the top of the bowl. Johnny Jorgensen says if the kid keeps ordering wood the way he has been that Johnny won't have to go fishing next year."

Kate thought of the last time she'd seen Bill, Johnny's brother, and said, "That's okay, Bill's going to need to use the drift permit next summer to pay for his divorce anyway."

Bobby slapped the two halves of a bun together. "Here, put yourself on the outside of this."

Kate stretched her hand out and noticed in a detached sort of way that her hand was shaking too much to be able to grip the plate holding up her dinner.

"Woman, what in hell's wrong with you?" Bobby said. He tossed the plate down on the hearth and wheeled his chair over to grasp her cold hands firmly between his warm ones. "Who cares enough about a couple of lost Outsiders to make you shake this bad?"

"Somebody cared enough to take a shot at me outside the NorthCom shack," she said wearily, and to her horror felt tears sting her eyes.

"Well, now," Bobby said, startled. He tried to subdue his

natural roar and almost succeeded. "That's what Abel meant, about getting you here safe?"

She nodded, unable to speak, and Bobby scooted closer to the couch. He grasped the arms of his chair and in one smooth, economical movement swung himself over beside her. He put his arms around her and she subsided gratefully into his embrace. They sat like that for some time. Bobby rubbed her back and murmured soothing nothings and Kate gradually regained her composure. When he felt the worst of her trembling fade away he pulled back to look her over critically. "I think this is one time you could use a little something extra in your coffee." He leaned forward to reach beneath the seat of his chair.

She shook her head, warding off the bottle of Wild Turkey. "I'll be all right."

"Hell yes, you'll be all right," he said, the roar back. He topped off his own mug, took a big swallow, and topped it off again. "It's not as if the both of us ain't been shot at before."

She gave him a half-smile. "Right."

"Question is, which dumb fucker's doing the shooting this time?"

She got up and refilled her coffee mug, cooling it off with evaporated milk and sweetening it with two teaspoons of sugar. Bobby's coffee would dissolve the lining in your stomach if you didn't doctor it up. "I think it was my cousin Martin."

"What!" This time his roar brought Mutt to her feet, ears straight up, ready to protect and defend. Kate soothed her with a quick word. "Do you mean to sit there and tell me that that pimply-assed, gook-faced, chickenshit excuse for a man actually had the gumption to use you for target practice?" She nodded, and Bobby grinned. "I never thought he had it in him."

"Me either," she said.

Bobby thought about it for a while, before cocking an eyebrow at Kate. "He's a good shot, drunk or sober, is that ole boy," he said. "I been duck hunting with him."

"I know. So have I."

"Means if he missed you he meant to."

"I know that, too."

"This is taking sibling rivalry a little bit too far," he observed.

"Don't I know it," she said ruefully.

He hoisted himself back into his chair and whipped it around until they were eyeball to eyeball. "Okay, sweetheart, tell Poppa all about it."

She told him everything, clearly and concisely. She took him back over all of it—Jack's visit, the suit named Gamble, first Miller and then Ken's disappearance, Bernie's odd liking for the little ranger and his account of the fight between Xenia's brother and Xenia's lover, the NorthCom operator's failure to make Miller's call for him, the strange case of the disappearing and reappearing Toyota, the shots in the dark, the truck on the bridge. It was only when she came to Xenia's part of the story that she edited the tale, some perverse spark of family loyalty rearing its head, but she knew from the look he gave her that Bobby was perfectly capable of filling in the blanks. By the time she finished, her burger was stone cold and his, still on the grill, was a crisp, charred shadow of its former self. Her stomach growled, but she had lost her appetite.

Bobby was frowning. "So you think Martin killed Miller and dumped him over the Lost Chance Creek bridge?"

"I'm not sure," Kate said, her brow creased. Bobby looked askance. "I know what you're thinking and, yes, Martin

Shugak's very existence is a bane on the community. He's been in and out of jail once or twice a year ever since he turned eighteen. He's been accused of everything from statutory rape to bootlegging to aggravated assault to hunting grizzly without a permit." Kate paused for breath, and added, "I just don't know if he killed the ranger."

"Why not?"

"He won that fight at the Roadhouse," Kate said simply. "All the time we were growing up, I don't remember Martin, with all his faults, ever repeating himself."

"And what was it he dumped off the Lost Chance Creek bridge if it wasn't a body?"

"I didn't say it wasn't a body," Kate retorted. "I just don't know whose."

"If he didn't kill the ranger, why would he be shooting at you?"

Kate smiled grimly. "You know what the bush telegraph is like, Bobby, you help run it yourself. I've been here almost a whole day, asking questions. Some of it was bound to get back to him. If he knows I've talked with Bernie, he knows that I know he's got a motive."

"If today's one of his few good days and he's sober enough to think at all."

"Mmm." She paused, and said, "I wish I knew who Miller wanted to call that night."

"His father," Bobby said.

Kate, surprised, said, "What?"

"He wanted to call his father in Washington, D.C. I didn't realize the guy was a congressman," Bobby added regretfully, as one who had lost a golden opportunity for some federal tit for tat. Bobby and the IRS had never really gotten along.

"Bobby," Kate said, sitting up straight, "I just came from

the NorthCom shack. The operator said that on that night the dish was down and he had messages backed up for twenty-four hours' worth of sending. He said Miller left without even filling out a form for the waiting list."

"That's right," Bobby said, nodding. "He came here."

"He what!"

"You lose your hearing between now and a second ago? He came here," Bobby repeated, patiently for him.

"You jackass, why didn't you tell me this before?"

"You jackass, because you didn't tell me he went missing that selfsame night before!" Bobby roared.

Kate, staring at him, realized her mouth was open and closed it. "Oh."

"'Oh,'" Bobby mimicked her. "'Oh' is right."

"So Miller came here and asked you to get a message to his father?" Kate said meekly. "What did he say to him?"

"I don't know's how I want to tell you," Bobby said, very huffy.

Kate gave him one of her better smiles, all sweet seduction and charm, a smile that would have made Chopper Jim proud. Bobby swallowed hard, and said gruffly, "He wanted to call his father in Washington, the Dick Capital of the world, so I called a ham I talk to in Georgetown."

"Did you listen to the conversation?"

"Sure, the ham has to stand by, Kate," he said. "Whoever talks on my radio is talking on my license, you know that."

"What was the conversation about?"

He drained his mug and looked sadly into its empty depths. Kate rose smartly to refill it. She poked around in the cupboards for a bag of Dare maple cookies, arranged them on a plate and set it where he could reach it without stretching. Watching her, Bobby grinned a little. Catching him, Kate grinned back.

Bobby laughed, shook his head and bit into a cookie, washing it down with coffee. Through the crumbs he said thickly, "He was telling his father about this old gold mine Mac Devlin wants to file on. I can't remember the name of the mine, but—"

"The Nabesna," Kate said.

"That's the one," Bobby said, snapping his fingers. "How'd you know?"

"Mac was telling me something about it earlier this evening. What else did Miller say?"

"Said he didn't think Devlin should be allowed to take over the mine, said he was sending some samples to Anchorage and that if they panned out he thought the government should lease out the diggings to a contractor and use the proceeds to finance Park development."

"Did Mac Devlin know the kid was trying to put him into competition with the federal government on this mine?"

Bobby shrugged. "You ask me, I'd say the kid had no secrets. He told everyone what he wanted to do in the Park, and when some of them disagreed, he said straight out, five by five, how stupid he thought they were." His mouth turned down at the corners. "He just couldn't understand why they weren't all on his side in the first place."

"Did he say where he was going after he left here?"

"Nope."

"Did he have his Toyota?"

"Yeah."

"You watched him leave?" Kate persisted. "You actually saw him in the Toyota when he left?"

"I was watching from the door," Bobby said, spacing his words out painstakingly. "I saw him get into his Toyota Land Cruiser and drive off toward Niniltna, yes. I'm crippled, Kate, not blind."

Oblivious, Kate asked, "How about Ken Dahl? Did he show up here asking questions about Miller?"

"You should have been a cop, Kate," Bobby said in a disgusted voice.

"I was, once. Have you seen him?"

Bobby shook his head. "Nope. Not since the potlatch last spring."

Kate linked her hands behind her head and stared into the fire. "So Miller called his dad." If Miller had called his father the night he disappeared, then his father had undoubtedly informed the FBI of it. And if the FBI knew, Gamble knew. It followed that Gamble must certainly have told Jack Morgan. But it wasn't in the file he had left on her kitchen table. She felt the anger well up inside her in a scalding wave and was glad of it. She wanted to stay angry with Jack and he was making it so easy for her. "Son of a bitch," she said quietly.

Bobby stared at her. "I beg your pardon?"

"That son of a *bitch*," Kate elucidated.

"Okay," Bobby said hastily, seeing the wrath gathering in her light brown eyes, and wondering how the rage of a woman five feet tall was able to scare him the way no VC ever had. "Not my business. I understand."

"I want to make a call myself," Kate said. "To Jack in Anchorage. Can do?"

"Sure," he said. "Tonight, if you want. KL7CC's always awake."

"No, the morning will do fine."

"No swearing on the air this time," he said sternly. "The FCC's been on my ass enough lately as it is; I don't need some YL fucking up my airwaves."

Kate sat in thought, her brow wrinkled. He watched her for a few moments, before turning to grill more burgers to replace the two congealing on the hearth. They ate, Bobby ravenously, Kate with more determination than pleasure. Kate looked up from licking her fingers to find Bobby fixing her with his bright gaze. She smiled at him, this time putting her heart into it. "May I stay the night?"

He brightened instantly. "Hot damn, am I about to get lucky?"

She looked at him and knew a sudden, overwhelming desire to be held, to be petted, to be taken up the mountain and shown the view, to sleep afterward secure and undisturbed in the arms of a friend she trusted absolutely and without reservation.

She was mightily tempted, and he saw it in her face. His smile was half-tender, half-mocking, and all male. "No go?"

She rose and stretched and patted his cheek. "You got lucky six years ago, Bobby. So did I. Let's don't tempt fate."

"Let's do," Bobby replied promptly, and they both laughed. "It's that fucker Morgan, ain't it?" he said shrewdly.

She gave him a look that should have frosted his socks. "I haven't seen Jack—in that way—in more than a year."

Unfrosted and unabashed, Bobby said, "Yeah, that's right, you been screwing that dumb fuck from Bahstahn, where they pahk the cahs and go to Hahvahd. You've done better, Kate."

Her spine became so straight and rigid that for a moment he thought it might snap. Her words came out measured and precise. "I will take the couch, thank you."

He surveyed her from beneath raised eyebrows. "Damn straight you're taking the couch. The only bed's mine."

Her eyes narrowed. "Don't push your luck, Bobby."

"I got nothing to lose, Katie," he said, grinning, and popped two wheelies on the way to bed, just to show her.

CHAPTER 7

JACK MORGAN STOOD PATIENTLY while the tribal council examined the Cessna he'd flown in on, the bag in his hand and the pockets of his parka. He understood the reasons for the search; he even approved of them.

A year before, Niniltna's tribal council had taken a long, hard look at the last ten years' worth of alcohol-related murders, rapes, wife beatings and child abuse and had gone damp. Specifically, you could drink alcohol in the privacy of your own home, but you couldn't buy anything stronger than orange juice. Having alcohol in your possession required careful thought and long-distance planning, however, because if you were caught buying or selling alcohol in any form to anyone of any age or race or faith within tribal boundaries, the council sicked Kate Shugak on you, and if that happened, as Sandy Halvorsen had been heard to say on his way out of the Park, "you might as well be dead, because you'll wish you were." Sandy Halvorsen had been the latest in a long line of Park bootleggers. The latest and, so far, the last.

On the airstrip it was your choice. If you didn't like the law, you and your plane could leave without being searched and don't come back, thank you very much, and there was a ring of tribal councillors, each with their very own 12-gauge, standing in a line between your plane and their town, just in case you got cute. Jack stood where he was and endured the patting down of his body and the shakedown of his plane. Kate was waiting for him at the side of the strip.

She was alone. Abel had materialized at Bobby's door immediately after Bobby had put her call through to Jack. It took a judicious application of the best coffee in the Park and dogged perseverance to persuade the old man to allow her to meet Jack alone. She left Mutt behind, too. She wanted privacy for this encounter, with no inhibitors present to cramp her style.

Jack passed his frisk and was waved through. "You knew the kid called his father the night he disappeared!" she flung at him when he was still twelve feet away.

"No," he said, in his deep, calm voice.

"You knew about the mine, too!"

"Gamble knew, Kate. I didn't."

"You *knew* Devlin had a motive to get rid of the kid! Goddam you, Jack! You want me to clean up your mess and you won't give me what I need to do it! I ought to—"

Jack sighed and dropped his grip onto the packed snow of the landing strip. "Kate, just shut up for a minute and listen to me. Gamble didn't tell me the kid called his father the night he disappeared, or at least he didn't until we were back in Anchorage. He says there was some foul-up between Washington and the branch office in Seattle, but I figure Miller Senior didn't want his name on an FBI file."

"You son of a bitch," Kate said, not listening. She felt suddenly, gloriously angry. He looked up and caught her expression and took an involuntary step backward. "You son of a bitch. You sent me in blind." He saw the swing coming and caught her fist in one hand. "You sent me in here blind, the same way you did when you sent me out on that squeal fourteen months ago." She kicked out at his shin and caught him sharply just above his right boot.

"Ouch!" he yelped, dropping her hand for his shin.

"You knew these guys weren't just missing!" She swung and missed. "You knew you were sending me into trouble!" She swung and connected with a lucky one just above his belt.

Air whoofed out of him. "Goddamit, Kate," he gasped, "cut it out!" He grabbed her arms and lifted her out of reach.

"Investigation in progress, you said," she sneered. "We've only got the neighbor's statement, you said. Probably nothing at all, but we've got to check it out and you're up next."

He paled beneath his beard. "Do you think I would have sent you there alone if I'd known?"

"No warning, no backup, nothing!" she tried to shout, only the scar on her throat wouldn't let her. "For seven years I did every dirty job you gave me. Seven years of talking kids into testifying against their parents, wives against their husbands, sisters against their brothers and uncles. 'You're a woman, Kate,'" she said, mimicking his low drawl, "'you're a woman and you're from the bush and you know more than any Outsider could possibly know about how these people live.'"

Fourteen months of suffering dark dreams in the dead of night, of waking dreams every day, of remembering the curious ripping sound a knife made in human skin, especially curious when the skin was your own, of trying to forget the sight of a naked child fighting with her bare hands to protect her father from Kate, the sound of the high, thin childish voice imploring, begging, pleading for it all to stop, for it all just to stop, the feeling of triumph that had overwhelmed her in a fierce, rejoicing, hideous tide when she surfaced to realize she was upright with the perp's knife in her hand, bleeding but alive, as he lay in front of her with his intestines and his life oozing out of him, and the child, always the child, crying in the back of her mind. Waking, sleeping, working at rest, Kate knew with a dreadful certainty that she would never be able to forget the long, silent tears sliding down the cheeks of the naked, bleeding child.

For fourteen months she had said nothing, had blunted every effort by every friend she had to get at the hurt, had pushed back the reckoning, and now here he was, Jack Morgan, her nemesis, her fate, the man who had hired her to deal every day of her working life with hurt, terrified, defenseless children, who had loved her and asked, no, demanded that she love him in return, who had taken her rejection of himself, his job, his love and his world without apparent objection, who hadn't so much as winced when she took up with his subordinate. She let him have it, all the bitterness, all the pain, the rejection and the guilt, fourteen months of it, a lifetime of it. She was powerless to stop the flow, and she wouldn't have if she could.

Jack stood with his head down as the flood poured over him, unsmiling, his blue eyes unflinching. With every accusation and condemnation she shouted at him in her hoarse, ragged voice, deep down inside his gut he heard a full orchestra sounding another verse of the "Hallelujah Chorus."

"If I'd tried to take that job away from you, you would have castrated me or quit," he said softly when at last the worst of the flood had passed. "You were good at it, Kate. You were the best."

"Yeah, well, I'm not much good for anything now, thanks to you."

"Don't be silly, Kate."

"Don't tell me what or what not to do," she said, flaring up again. "The day is long past when I listen to anything you have to say."

"Then be as silly as you want," he said in that same soothing voice, and she eyed him resentfully.

"Prick," she said with deep loathing.

He gave her a sudden grin that was as unexpected as it was dangerously contagious. "Feel better?"

"Fuck off!" she said through her teeth.

"You feel better," he decided. "Let's go find Mac Devlin."

• • •

They found Mac Devlin the first place they looked, with his feet up on Billy Mike's desk. He was expounding at length on the future joys in store for Niniltna when Devlin Mining gained all its Mickey Mouse government permits and—Billy would forgive him for saying it—rid itself of all the Mickey Mouse aboriginal mining restrictions as well. When Devlin Mining moved into full production—well.

Mac was picking a date on which to take the company public with a stock issue that would unquestionably be listed on the Big Board within hours after its release when Kate and Jack walked in. Billy Mike was listening with an expression of saintly resignation. Kate didn't fool herself for a moment that the pleasure with which the tribal chief greeted her and Jack had anything to do with how glad he was to see them. He bustled out from behind his desk, interrupting Mac in mid-oration, and grasped both their hands enthusiastically. He was a rotund little man with shiny black hair. He wore a shiny black suit to match, with a string tie drawn through a large, ornately carved and colored piece of ivory that looked as if it were holding up his chin.

Billy Mike was fifty-five years old. Born in Niniltna back when Alaska was still only a territory, he had never been farther away from home than Anchorage. He'd been elected tribal chief only when Ekaterina Shugak declined to continue representing the Niniltna Native Association at the annual Alaska Federation of Natives meetings. He embraced Alaska and the Park with an abiding and inarticulate devotion, he loved his wife and their seven children, he was happy and contented in his job, and he rejoiced openly in his good fortune without the slightest trace of smugness. Spending more than thirty consecutive minutes in Billy Mike's company made Kate feel suicidal.

It didn't help that almost all of his seven children had been, were now going or would be going to the University of Alaska, Fairbanks, where they would major in business administration in order to learn how to run the Niniltna Native Association when their father went on to his no doubt just reward. It was a given, like death or taxes, and six of his children understood that perfectly. The seventh, born male and afflicted with the name Dandy, was suspended for a year from school when he was caught with a retail-size marijuana crop in his second-floor room in UAF's Lathrop dormitory. He was serving his sentence at home, making his life a burden unto his father by hanging out with Martin Shugak. Kate remembered this interesting piece of information at almost the same instant she remembered seeing him at the Roadhouse the night before, exiting the back end of a pickup with his jeans down around his ankles.

She smiled at his father. "So what're you up to lately, Billy?"

"Oh, about two hundred and forty pounds, Kate," he said comfortably, and showed them to seats. "Can I pour you some coffee?"

Kate refused, Jack accepted and Billy bustled around filling mugs. There was some conversation about the summer's catch, the fall hunt and the current cold snap. The mugs were refilled and Kate got down to business. "Actually, Billy," she said, "we've been looking for Mac. We'd like to talk to him. Would it be all right if we used a room here in the building?"

Billy had a lively sense of self-preservation and recognized an escape when it hit him over the head. He stood up again at once. "Use my office, Kate. No, really, it's okay, it's my pleasure."

"Hey, Billy—" Mac began to say.

"No, I've got a meeting down the hall anyway." Billy disappeared with a wave of his hand.

Mac Devlin raised his eyebrows over merry brown eyes. "The granddaughter of Ekaterina Shugak speaks, and the earth moves. Or in this case, those on it."

"Where were you the night of October 26?" Kate said bluntly.

The brown eyes became less merry and the burly body stiffened in its chair. "Why?"

"Because that was the night Mark Miller disappeared."

Mac looked from Kate to Jack and back again. "Why would you think I might have anything to do with that?"

"It's too late to play coy, Mac. Because you knew Miller was going to call his daddy in Washington, D.C., and try to cross you up getting permits for the Nabesna Mine. You knew about it, didn't you, Mac? Everybody knew about it; God knows Miller made no secret of it, but you had the most to lose if it happened. First he calls the EPA in on your operation on Carmack Creek, then he gets in between you and the Nabesna Mine." She rose to her feet and circled around his chair. Mac's head swiveled to follow her. "The kid was smart, he had ideas, and then he had that father of his, and you knew the only thing that could stop him was if he were stopped permanently. So you killed him."

"Well, now, Kate," Jack said soothingly, "maybe we should go easy on poor old Mac. I can understand how a man might be upset that his life's work was on the line like that. It was probably just an accident."

"Accident, my ass! Miller's been missing for six weeks and no one's found his body. That doesn't sound like an accident to me."

"I'm sure Mac didn't really mean to hurt anybody," Jack insisted.

"And what about Ken Dahl?" Kate said. "He get a little too close to the truth maybe, huh, Mac? So he had to go, too?"

Mac looked from her to Jack and back one more time, and said, "Give it a rest, guys."

Kate straightened and said sweetly, "But you so obviously expected us to sweat you, Mac. We couldn't disappoint you."

"You'd never have forgiven us," Jack added.

Jack chuckled. Kate chuckled. After a moment, Mac chuckled, too. The room reeked of good fellowship and bonhomie.

"So where were you October 26, Mac?" Jack asked, sounding reluctant but bound to do his duty. "You've got a motive, you're a suspect, you've got to account for your whereabouts that night."

Mac tossed off the rest of his coffee and got to his feet. "October 26 I was in Juneau." He surveyed their resulting reactions with satisfaction, and added gently, "At dinner with the governor, his wife, the lieutenant governor and his wife, and my date, a Melissa Fensterwald. She works for the Department of Natural Resources."

He stopped at the door and looked back at them. "You're right about one thing, Kate. That little prick Miller was going to spend the rest of his life trying to talk Park residents into his way of thinking. Development, yes, but limited development and run by the government for the specific purpose of increasing public access." He paused, and said, "What makes you think I've got a problem with that? If he offered me a big enough percentage I'd dig gold here for Moammar Kaddafi." His eyes met Kate's steadily. "Who wouldn't?"

Their gaze held for a long moment. Mac broke it off, and turned to leave. Kate stared after him with knitted brows. "Mac," she said suddenly.

He halted in the doorway. "What?"

"Did you talk to Ken Dahl two weeks ago? About Miller?"

"I did." Mac's merry brown gaze mocked her.

"What'd you tell him?"

Mac shrugged. "He'd heard I'd no cause to love the little prick. He wanted to know who else felt that way."

"What did you tell him?"

Mac rubbed his hand over his brush cut. "He wanted to know if I thought Miller's testimony before that House subcommittee could have had anything to do with his disappearance. I said it could have, but that I thought your cousin Martin's fight with Miller that night had more."

"And that's all?" Jack said.

Mac grinned, a hard, jolly grin. "I thought it was enough." From Kate's expression, he could see she thought it was enough, too, and he left with a jaunty step.

Jack flopped down in Mac's vacated chair. "We didn't ask him where he was when Ken disappeared."

"Nope."

"No need, I guess."

"Nope."

"Think we'd better verify his alibi?"

121

"Yup."

"Think it'll stand up?"

"Yup."

"Me, too," Jack said, slumping. "Gamble's hanging around Anchorage with nothing to do. I'll put him on it, get him to call Juneau in the morning."

"So. Where does that leave us?"

"With Martin," Jack said. "I'm sorry, Kate, but he's all we have left."

She rubbed one hand over her face. "I know he's my cousin, Jack, and I'm supposed to be biased. But I still don't think he did it."

After seven years of working with her and five years of loving her, Jack Morgan had learned to respect Kate Shugak's hunches. Still, he was going to make her flesh it out, or try to. "Why not?"

She was silent, and then she said in a voice so low he could barely hear it, "Because my grandmother wants me to think he did."

"What?"

"She pointed me toward Xenia the moment I got here. She knows everything that goes on all over the Park, so she must have known Xenia was seeing Miller, and that Martin and Miller fought over it at the Roadhouse."

"Maybe she's trying to help us find Miller."

Kate looked at Jack with wise and suddenly very old eyes, and for a fleeting moment he felt reduced to the size and age of a first-grader. "Jack, you've known Ekaterina for—what?—five, six years, now? Don't kid yourself that you *know* her. You've only seen what she wants you to see. The neat old lady holding friends and family together against the pressures of modern life. The upright tribal leader guiding her people out

122

of the wilderness and into parity with the twentieth century. The profile in the *Anchorage Daily News*. You've never been face to face with the real Ekaterina Moonin Shugak."

"And who is the real Ekaterina Moonin Shugak?" he asked in an indulgent voice.

She shook her head, unsmiling. "The real Ekaterina Moonin Shugak could give Niccolò Machiavelli lessons. She's arrogant, manipulative and very, very powerful. Make no mistake, Jack, she runs this town, in spirit if not in name. She practically runs the Park. She could run the Alaska Federation of Natives if she wanted to, and as it is the president of AFN flies in once a month to consult with her."

Startled, Jack said, "I didn't know that."

"The governor himself asked her to mediate that land swap between the state and Kachemak, Inc." Kate smiled at Jack's expression. "Oh yes, Jack. Billy Mike might be tribal chief in name, but she is in fact and he knows it. He won't make a move without her backing him every step of the way." Kate shivered and rubbed her hands over her arms. She could not remember another winter this cold. "And I've got a feeling she doesn't want that ranger or whatever's left of him found."

"Why?"

"I don't know yet."

"Maybe because she doesn't want Xenia hurt," he suggested.

It was her turn to look indulgent. "She's doing her -damndest to see that none of Xenia's generation ever leaves the Park, and she's driving Xenia crazy in the process." She was silent for a moment. She looked up at him with a twisted smile. "She approves of you, did you know?"

"Xenia?"

"Emaa. She thinks you are a good man. She even manages

to call you by name." She saw his look and said, "Don't knock it. It's more than she was ever able to do for Ken."

He stared at her for a long moment, and swiveled around to look away from her. "Great," he said under his breath. "That's just great."

"What?" Kate said.

"Nothing," he said lightly, lying through his teeth. "I'm honored."

She laughed shortly. "You should be." She picked up her parka. "I'm going out to the Roadhouse." Jack's face lost some of its normally healthy ruddiness. Kate paused with her hand on the doorknob and said maliciously, "Well? Are you coming?"

"Why do we have to go to the Roadhouse?"

"Because, at this time of year it's the one place we're sure to find Martin. It's more than time we stopped talking about him and started talking to him."

He hesitated.

"We'd better get going, Jack. If I know Abel, we're not going to be able to dodge him for much longer."

"Why do we have to dodge him at all?"

"Because if he knew what we know, Abel's just the guy to prune the Park of one Martin Ivanovich Shugak."

She held the door open, waiting. Giving her a damning glare, he grabbed his parka and stamped past her.

• • •

To get from Niniltna to the river road that led to the Roadhouse, for the first mile or so they had to follow the old roadbed of the Kanuyaq River & Northern Railroad to Lost Chance Creek. A few hundred yards beyond the Lost Chance, the road to Bernie's branched off to the right while the railroad bed turned left to climb into the Quilaks. But first, always, and forever, you had to cross the creek.

Lost Chance Creek was at the bottom of a gorge that ran for three miles upstream and two down. It could not be got around, or tunneled beneath; it had to be crossed over, and to do that the Kanuyaq River & Northern Railroad had built a trestle and run tracks across it. The tracks were long gone, but the trestle remained, impervious to all the abuse heaped upon it by sixty Alaskan winters. It now supported the comings and goings of the Park residents on trucks and snow machines with the same reliability it had supported railcars carrying over half a million tons of copper and a billion ounces of silver. The trestle was seven hundred feet long and narrow enough that you didn't want to open the doors of your pickup when you were crossing it. It had no railings, on either side.

What concerned Jack Morgan most was that it was three hundred feet high.

They roared up to Lost Chance Creek on Kate's snow machine. Kate stopped well before the bridge, and waited, letting the engine idle. The snow machine shifted as Jack climbed off, and without looking around Kate gunned the throttle and sped across the bridge. On the other side, she stopped again. This time she shut off the machine and got off. She fussed with the gas cap and the throttle, biding her time, before she looked back.

Jack was on his hands and knees, his nose practically touching the hard-packed snow beneath him, his eyes never looking to the right or to the left but only straight down at the tracks left by the treads of countless snow machines. He was crawling directly down the center of the bridge.

It should have been a sight to delight Kate's soul. She

strolled to the edge of the gorge and peered over the side. Three weeks until Christmas and Lost Chance Creek still ran free, the white water moving at breakneck speed over a jumble of fallen rocks, splintered trunks of deadfall, remnants of eroded banks. Ice crusted thickly on whatever the spray touched.

It took Jack eleven minutes to cross the bridge. Kate was counting. He didn't get up from all fours until he was at least twenty feet onto the access. He rose, dusted off his mittens and the knees of his down overalls and for the first time saw her standing on the edge of the precipice. Returning color was immediately washed out of his face. "What the hell do you think you're doing?" he shouted. His bass voice echoed faintly off the walls of the gorge.

She turned, facing him fully, standing with the heels of her shoepacs an inch from the edge, and said, her hands in her pockets, "Looking for bodies."

"There'll be one more if you don't watch your ass, Shugak!"

She shrugged and turned back to look into the gorge. There wasn't anything to see and she knew it, but she took her time looking anyway. A movement caught the corner of her eye and she glanced up to see a bald eagle back-winging down to settle in the very top of a spruce tree. They looked at each other in silence, an odd similarity in the ferocity of their expressions.

Jack stood where he was, his urge to snatch her from the brink of the abyss and his fear of the abyss itself warring clearly in his face. Kate waited for another minute, counting one-Mississippi to herself, before sauntering back to the snow machine and climbing on. "Coming?" she said over her shoulder.

Jack climbed back on behind Kate without a word. His

eyes met her own calmly enough, but he couldn't hide the sheen of sweat on his forehead or the gray slowly receding from his complexion. She wondered suddenly if she'd been born a brass-plated bitch or if she'd just grown that way, and when. "Okay?" she said in a voice more gentle than he'd heard in fourteen months.

"Okay," he said. She smiled at him, and his eyes widened. "It walks, it talks, it smiles," he said his voice marveling. "It might even be human." Kate's smile vanished and he added, his voice caressing, "On my way over I was remembering the first time we crossed that bridge together." He grinned. "I was remembering how you cured my vertigo then."

She jerked the snow machine around and hit the gas, so that Jack almost pulled her off when he grabbed her waist. Even so, she felt him shaking with laughter all the way to Bernie's.

There was a party of Dall sheep hunters from somewhere Outside shucking their gear in front of the Roadhouse, being shepherded through the process by Demetri Totemoff. Kate pulled up to one side, killed the motor and pocketed the keys. She stood up, stripping the hood of her snowsuit back, and walked toward the door of the Roadhouse, Jack following.

One of the hunters stepped into Kate's way. She looked up, surprised. "How," the man said, holding his hand up, palm out.

"Oh, Jesus," she heard Demetri say. She felt Jack pause behind her.

"Me no talk white man talk," Kate said pleasantly. "Now get the fuck out of my way." She shoved him and his fading smile to one side and went up the steps.

Inside the Roadhouse Kate was underwhelmed to find not only Martin but Xenia as well, sitting at opposite ends of the bar and pointedly ignoring each other. Kate muttered something under her breath that Jack didn't catch, and went over to take Xenia by the elbow. She deposited the girl at a table, and went for the girl's brother.

"Well, hey, Katya," Martin said, a six-pack shy of passing out. "What you doing here? I thought you sweared off the Park for good when you busted Sandy."

"I thought so too, Martin," she said grimly, steering him to the table where an imperturbable Jack and an apprehensive Xenia waited for them.

Before Kate had seated herself Xenia burst out, "You said you wouldn't tell him! You promised!"

"I lied," Kate said. "Watch out she doesn't bolt," she said to Jack. "She does that a lot." She turned to Martin. "Martin," she said, trying to get him to focus on her. "Martin?"

Martin Shugak was tall for an Aleut, but in everything else he was a carbon copy of his sister, with perhaps a more stubborn chin. He sported a wispy mustache and goatee that made him look like Fu Manchu and long, lank hair reaching his shoulders that might have been washed sometime within the last decade but didn't look or smell like it. His clothes were in even worse shape, and Kate only just managed to stop herself from moving her chair farther away from his. Her nose would adjust in a moment, she knew from long experience.

Martin had left the eighth grade when his father drowned, to take over fishing his father's permit in Prince William Sound. While the salmon ran he was sober, hardworking and solvent. The other seven months of the year he drank up what he had earned during the previous five. There was no cannery in Cordova who would not finance a new boat for Martin Shugak the first week of May. There was no cannery in Cordova who would advance him a dime after October.

His eyes wavered around the room and eventually came to rest on her face. "Katya," he said, a foolish smile crossing his face, "what you doing here? I thought—"

"Yeah, yeah," Kate said impatiently, "you thought I swore off the Park. Martin, do you remember Mark Miller?"

"Who?"

"Mark Miller, the park ranger."

Martin made a face. "Doan know him. How 'bout 'nother beer?"

"Bernie!" Bernie looked up and Kate circled her forefinger in the air. Bernie nodded and a moment later brought over three Olys and a Coke. Martin grabbed for his and sucked half down thirstily.

Kate wrestled the bottle out of his hand and held it out of his reach. "You know Miller, Martin. The park ranger who was going out with Xenia."

Martin's brow furrowed in deep thought. "Xenia."

"Your sister," Kate specified.

Martin transferred his wavering gaze to his sister's pinched face, and frowned. "I remember."

"Thank God," Jack said to Kate. "I thought for a second we were going to have to introduce them."

"Little bastard," Martin said, unheeding. "Told him to leave my sister alone." He brightened. "Beat the shit out of him, too. Candy-ass."

"Then what did you do?" Kate said. "After you beat the shit out of him."

He looked at her, surprised. "Went home, I guess."

"Have you seen him since?"

"Nope." He snickered. "Probly hiding."

"He's been missing for six weeks, Martin, and you had a fight with him just hours before nobody ever saw him again."

129

"So what?" Martin said, seeming a little surprised that Kate would waste both their time remarking on it. "Good riddance, I'd say."

Kate reached over and grabbed Martin's face with both hands, trying to penetrate the alcoholic fog with sheer force of will. "I'll tell you what we think happened, Martin. Xenia was dating him and you didn't like it. She said he was going to marry her and take her away from the Park, and you didn't believe him or her. You argued with him about it. Half the crowd at Bernie's heard you say you were going to kill him if he didn't stay away from her."

"Aw shit, Kate," Martin said, looking everywhere but at her face. "Aw shit."

"So you did. You left Bernie's and you waited till he came out and you killed him, and then you rolled his body into Lost Chance Creek off the old railroad bridge."

Martin blinked. "What you say?"

"Martin, Xenia saw you do it. She recognized your truck, she saw the license plate and the expired sticker and the dented fender. She heard the splash when the body went in."

"Xenia?" Martin said, sitting up straight and suddenly more sober than he had been all week. "Body? Kate, what the hell are you talking about?"

"I'm talking about the park ranger you dumped over the Lost Chance bridge Thursday night, October 26, an hour after you fought with Miller right here in this bar."

Martin stared from Kate to Xenia to Jack and back to Kate. "I didn't kill no park ranger."

"Prove it," Kate said.

"I didn't kill nobody," Martin said doggedly. His eyes lit on Xenia and brightened. He pointed at his sister and said, "Xenia probably killed him because he wasn't going to marry

130

up with her and take her out of the Park like he said."

Xenia reached across the table to grab a hank of Martin's hair in one fist and begin beating on him with the other. The table rocked, the drinks spilled in everyone's laps, and Martin and Xenia rolled onto the floor, hissing and spitting and biting and scratching. When Jack and Kate finally got them separated Martin was missing a hank of hair above his left ear and Xenia's right eye was swelling shut.

"Sit down, Xenia," Kate said tightly. "I said sit down!" She slung the girl into a seat as Jack righted a chair and jammed Martin into it. "I'm having a good time," he told Kate. "Are you having a good time?" Activity in the Roadhouse barely checked. Bernie brought over another round, and peace if not serenity reigned supreme once more.

"If you didn't kill the ranger, Martin," Kate said, "then whose body were you dumping into Lost Chance Creek that night?"

"Aw shit, Kate," Martin said, "it wasn't nobody's body, it was a goddam moose."

There was a stunned silence. He looked from Kate's face to Jack's and back again. He hung his head and admitted, "It was a yearling female. I shot it up on the Kanuyaq around Silver Creek and I was bringing it home when Dandy told me there was a fish hawk in town. I wasn't going back to jail for no goddam moose." Kate met his eyes, and he slammed down his beer indignantly. "Jesus, Kate, if you won't believe me, ask Dandy, he was with me, he'll tell you."

Kate was silent for a moment. "Where were you last night about nine o'clock?"

Martin thought hard about this, his brow furrowed. Realization was long in coming, but when it did, his face flushed. He looked from his cousin to his sister with an expression half-guilty, half-pleading. "Oh," he said. "That."

"Yes," Kate said dryly, "that. You could have killed me."

"Aw shit, Katya," Martin said, "you know I can put a bullet wherever I want."

"Yes, well," Kate said, "why shoot at me at all?"

"I wan't—wasn't shooting at you," he insisted. "I dint even know you was there." He waved his hands expressively in the air. "I was just...you know, aiming in the general direction of the NorthCom shack. She"—he hooked his thumb toward Xenia—"keeps picking up these little bastards and I keep having to scare them off. I tell you, Katya," Martin said with a martyred air, "I tell you, it's a full-time job being Xenia's brother."

Kate gave Xenia a long look and said, "I can understand that, Martin. It's a full-time job being her cousin."

"Yeah," Martin said with deep fellow feeling. "So anyway, no hard feelings about last night, right, Kate?"

"No, no hard feelings, Martin," Kate said, and added casually and cruelly, "I can't speak for Abel, of course."

Martin's face lost its alcoholic flush and went a little gray. "Jesus Christ, Kate, was that who that was with you?"

Kate nodded.

Martin licked his lips, and braced himself. "He know it was me?"

Kate smiled.

Martin swallowed, tried to speak, went red, then white, shoved himself upright and staggered back to the bar. Xenia, ignoring everyone, flounced over to another table and proved how unconcerned she was with Kate's opinion by drinking a great deal of beer and talking loudly and laughing often.

Jack sat back and nursed his beer. "Well?"

"I love my family," Kate said, her voice grim.

"Besides that."

"He's telling the truth," she said flatly.

Jack sighed. "Yeah." There was a brief silence. He thought of something else and brightened. "This means we don't have to climb down into the Lost Chance gorge, doesn't it?"

Kate managed a mirthless smile. "As soon as we find Dandy Mike and he confirms Martin's story, that's what it means."

"That's what I thought it meant," Jack said in a satisfied voice. "Does Abel know it was Martin who shot at you two last night?"

"Not yet."

Jack finished off his beer and rose to his feet. "Oh, Katie, you can be such a hard-nosed bitch."

She batted her eyelashes at him. "You do say such sweet things, Jack honey."

CHAPTER 8

BOBBY WAS IN THE process of negotiating a fee, to be paid in moose steaks, for the broadcasting of a sale notice of Samuel Dementieff's last summer's red salmon gear. "Five roasts, not less than five pounds each," Bobby said in his usual roar, glaring at the elderly fisherman. "And don't think I won't weigh 'em, either."

Sam, seventy going on fifteen, glared right back and said fiercely, "Three, and you repeat the ad every night for a week."

"Four; and you get the weekend back-to-back special," Bobby said, leaning forward and glaring harder.

"Three," Sam said, leaning forward in turn, "and I'll throw in the tongue, and I get the weekend special and the week in between."

Mention of the tongue weakened Bobby visibly, as Sam had known it would. "And you play The Doors around it," he added. "I like 'Light My Fire.'" With gnarled hands he smoothed his cap on over his grizzled hair.

The deal was struck. It took them another ten minutes of haggling to compose the ad, and Bobby another five to pare it from a hundred words to fifty, each one of which Sam examined suspiciously and approved reluctantly, letter by letter. At the door he turned to fire his parting shot. "Starting tonight?"

"Will you get the hell out of here, you old pirate!" Bobby

yelled. Sam Dementieff smiled, a thin, triumphant smile, and swaggered out. "And what the hell do you want?"

This last was addressed to half a dozen teenagers loitering purposefully on the porch. The kids, three of whom Kate recognized as part of Bernie's first-string junior varsity girls' team, looked down at the snow melting on their boots and said nothing. "And get in here before you give the place a bad name," he added irritably with a slight reduction in decibels, but only slight, because he didn't want anyone ever to be able to say he was softening up in his old age. "Well? You there. You're Mike Kvasnikof's son, aren't you? Eknaty, isn't it?"

Mutely appealed to by his friends, Eknaty Kvasnikof hesitated and then said with a rush, "Mr. Clark, you know that commercial you're broadcasting for the bake sale the junior high class is having on Saturday at the gym?"

"What of it?" Bobby said. "It's on the spindle, I'll get to it in order tonight at eight when I go on the air. Get out."

Eknaty cast a wild eye about him for support. His friends looked at their feet, at the ceiling, out the window, anywhere but at Bobby or at anything that might draw Bobby's attention. Eknaty swallowed and said in a timid voice, "Well, when you do, we were wondering...maybe you could play some modern music before and after? Not too modern," he hastened to add. "Actually, it's kind of a classic."

Bobby snorted. "Mod-run music," he said, rolling his eyes at Kate, who had the temerity to laugh. "A classic, no less. Which?"

Eknaty reached beneath his parka and pulled out a copy of Michael Jackson's "Thriller."

There was an electric silence. Bobby's eyes bulged. Bobby's neck swelled. Bobby's black skin went blacker. Before he had one word out the kids were already trampling over themselves in their haste to get to the door, reminding Kate irresistibly of the scene at the Roadhouse the night before. A string of unprintables followed the stampede outside, and Bobby rolled over to the open door to roar after them, "Idjits! Any moron knows that any track recorded after Credence Clearwater broke up is noise ain't fit to inflict on a fruit bat! Now get the hell off the earth!"

He slammed the door so hard that the rafters rang, shutting out the faint cries of panic receding down the road, and threw back his head and laughed and laughed and laughed.

"Well," Jack remarked in an unruffled voice, "I guess it's Jim Morrison tonight and like it."

"How the hell are you, Morgan?" Bobby said, wiping away tears and sending his chair whizzing across the room.

Jack did a quick two-step to keep his toes out of range, and gripped Bobby's hand in a warm clasp. "Got a license yet for that broadcast of yours?"

"What broadcast?"

"You're nothing but a born-again outlaw, Clark," Jack said, and Bobby grinned hugely.

"Why, I thank you, Jack, I purely do. If you thought on it for a year, you couldn't have come up with a nicer compliment." He turned to look at Kate. "Abel stopped by on his way home this afternoon, Kate, and cussed you up one side and down the other." He sighed reminiscently and added, "I do love to hear that old man cuss. It's an art form, the way he puts four-letter words together."

"Oh hell. Why's he mad this time?" Kate said, sounding plaintive. "I haven't done anything lately."

Bobby grinned again, this time a wicked, evil grin. "Seems he found out who was shooting at you two last night." He watched Kate's expression change with evident satisfaction.

"Seems he thinks you knew all along it was Martin and didn't tell him just because you thought Abel might shoot him. I told him I couldn't believe you would think such a thing, since we all know what a mild temper he has, and he called me a—let me see, a black-faced, black-hearted Park parasite without the brains God give a lemming, and at that he thought he might be insulting the lemming."

"And?"

"And after that he got really nasty."

"Where is he now?"

Bobby scratched his head. "From what I could make out, I think the idea was to go home and stay home for the rest of his natural life, and if somebody started shooting at you not to look for him to get in the way ever again."

"Good," Kate said fervently. "Let's hope he stays there this time. The third time's liable to be the charm for him taking my bullets."

"Maybe everybody's really been shooting at Abel, not you," Bobby suggested.

Kate yawned. "I wish."

It had been a long day, a longer week and the longest ever year, and the warmth of Bobby's fire and the comfort of Bobby's couch were siren songs too seductive to be ignored. She summoned up just enough energy to shrug out of her parka, kick off her shoepacs and stoke up the fireplace. With the men's voices a low, pleasant hum in the background and Mutt curled up on the floor next to her, she fell into a deep, dreamless sleep, not even waking when Jack drew a quilt over her.

• • •

The next morning Bobby raised KL7CC in Anchorage and got him to call Gamble. In an hour the FBI agent had confirmed Mac Devlin's alibi. By noon they had located Dandy Mike, in bed with one arm around Vic Porter's wife and the other around a fifth of Canadian Club. When they told him what they wanted, Dandy laughed so loud and so long they almost didn't bother confirming that it had been, indeed, a cow moose that had gone over the side of Lost Chance Creek bridge that dark night six weeks before.

Back at Bobby's house, Jack said, with more irritation than mystification, "If Martin didn't kill Miller like Xenia thought he did, and if Xenia didn't kill him like Martin thought she did, and if Devlin didn't kill him like we all wish he had, we're back to square one. We don't have any bodies, other than a bunch of dead moose that by now is probably too worn out to turn into steak." Jack appeared to regret the loss of the steak more than he regretted the loss of the culprit. "All we do have are, one, a park ranger, missing, and, two, the investigator I sent out after him, also missing." He looked up. "And that's it. There is no 'three.'"

"Why not just drop the whole thing?" Bobby said. "No Colonel Mustard in the drawing room with the wrench. No decaying bodies, no smoking guns, no crime to investigate. Why don't you just pack up and go home?"

"Gee, I'd love to," Jack said, "but the FBI and a United States congressman have different ideas. And there's the little matter of my own investigator's disappearance. Ken Dahl wasn't the kind of guy to vanish without a trace."

"Jimmy Hoffa's wife probably said pretty much the same thing about him," Bobby observed. "So what do we do now?"

Jack looked at him, alert and bright-eyed, and grinned inwardly. Bobby Clark, ace detective. "We go back to the beginning. First. I'm playing the devil's advocate here, but are we agreed that Miller is, in fact, dead?"

Kate said, "He hasn't been to work since October 26. His boss and his girl haven't seen him in six weeks, the same amount of time his Toyota's been sitting in front of Bernie's, in the process of being stripped down to its turn signal lever. His daddy hasn't seen him in six months. He hasn't called anybody, or written, or sent a message by jungle drums."

Jack gave a judicial nod. "So he's missing. Doesn't necessarily mean he's dead."

"Where's Ken Dahl?" Kate said bluntly.

"Maybe he fell down the same black hole swallowed up the ranger," Bobby suggested.

"Okay," Jack said, making a note and ignoring Bobby. "Then we assume for the sake of discussion that they are both dead, Miller we don't know why, Ken because he was looking for Miller. Second, we have motive for murder. Boy, do we have motive. Miller's testimony before that subcommittee was in favor of very limited development in the Park. As such it was bound to piss off everyone in the known world with the possible exception of Morris Udall. Even Bernie admits that Mark Miller was a good ranger with a lot of good ideas, but so is half the department. With his daddy in his corner, though, he had extra."

Jack stared at his notepad, frowning. "With his daddy backing him up he maybe had the stroke to push his ideas through. Not only that, but he dated Xenia and pissed off Martin. And Billy Mike tells us Miller also pissed off the tribal council for lecturing them on assigning the Qakiyaq Forest timber rights to an Oregon contractor without consulting with the council or making provisions for a training program for the locals. We know he pissed off Mac Devlin when he slapped an EPA injunction on him for fouling Carmack Creek with the sludge from his gold dredge, and then he started to get in Mac's way on the Nabesna mine deal." He sighed, and said, "We're just lousy with suspects, all with a surplus of motives."

"And all of whom have airtight alibis," Kate said morosely.

"That ranger boy just didn't have the knack of winning friends and influencing people, did he?" Bobby said. He was sitting very erect in his chair, his sharp black eyes darting from Kate to Jack and back again, enjoying all this detecting business immensely. "Hell, he even pissed old Abel off when he said at that hearing that the Park should be opened up to all tourists and not just those able to afford to fly in, and said the only way to do it was build and maintain a road with campsites and gas stations."

"Abel was there?" Kate said, startled.

"Hell, Kate," Bobby said, "Abel testified against the plans for development his own self."

Kate said, disbelieving, "Abel? Abel testified at the hearing?"

"Yes indeedy."

Awed, Kate said in a hushed voice, "What on earth did he say?"

Bobby put the tips of his fingers together and pursed his lips. "Well, first he stood up and said he'd been told the definition of a committee was a body with six heads and no brain and now he knew it was true. Then he sang 'em 'This Land is Your Land,' chorus and verse. Then he told 'em if they upgraded and maintained the road and put in campsites the tourists would come and ruin the natural grandeur of the park, preserving which, he reminded them, was what d-2 was all about." Bobby reflected, and added, "It was the best show I've seen since Wayne Newton's in Vegas."

Kate was laughing helplessly, tears rolling down her cheeks.

"'Course Abel didn't tell them he practically funded single-handedly the state's fight against d-2 when it was first proposed," Bobby added. "Sumbitch was starting to sound like he voted for Carter." He caught himself and gave Kate an apologetic look. "I don't mean to bad-mouth the old man any, Kate, but you ask other folks who was there and they'll tell you. That day Abel sounded green enough to sprout."

Kate wiped her eyes. "Oh Bobby. I will be sorry until the day I die I wasn't there to hear it."

"I, for one," Bobby said solemnly, hand on his heart, "shall always feel privileged that I was. It was a stirring example of democracy in action."

"So," Jack said, leading them relentlessly back to the main subject, "we're lousy with suspects who had beaucoup reasons to wish Miller had never been born."

"All of whom we've cleared," Kate reminded him, but she didn't sound as downcast about it as she had a half hour before.

"Maybe they all did it," Bobby said, inspired. "You know, like in *Murder on the Orient Express*. I got a copy of it around here somewhere if you want to read it."

"Let's try to give Miller's last known actions some kind of sequence," Jack said.

Bobby made a face. "Where were you at eight-oh-five and three seconds on the night in question? Bo-ring."

"Maybe. But it works. Got another piece of a paper? Thanks. Now, is it agreed that we follow the Miller trail on the assumption that Ken Dahl did the same; therefore, we follow one, we find them both?" He looked at Kate, and she nodded. "Okay. Miller began his day testifying before that Parks subcommittee. Next he goes to the NorthCom shack, all fired up to save the Nabesna mine from the evil machinations of that representative of Satan, that worthy heir to Snidely Whiplash, the one and only Mac Devlin. When he can't get a message to his daddy at NorthCom he comes here and talks to daddy over Bobby's radio. Afterward, he went to the Roadhouse, where he met Xenia and got into a fight with Martin. About what time would you say he left here, Bobby?"

Bobby shrugged. "I'd say around nine, but I wasn't keeping track."

"And he was driving his Toyota when he left. Okay. Now, Bernie says the Toyota was gone when he went to his house to grab a meal, so he was gone by midnight, and with what Bernie says about the fight, that more or less fits. But the Toyota was back in front of the Roadhouse by noon the next day." Jack looked up from his list. "What may we infer from that?"

There was silence. Kate said slowly, "That it was driven back to the Roadhouse by whoever killed Miller. Always assuming he was killed."

"I love a skeptic. Why?"

Kate sat forward, dark eyes intent. "That Land Cruiser would be like a red flag to anyone looking for Miller. The killer had to drive it somewhere else."

"And that means that he was in fact killed somewhere else," Bobby said with a burst of inspiration.

Jack bestowed a benevolent and approving smile on them both. "Very good."

"Now all we need," Kate said, sinking back into the couch, "is a witness who spent the hours between midnight on the twenty-sixth and noon on the twenty-seventh in front of the Roadhouse."

"Sober," Bobby added.

"Sober," Kate agreed. "And didn't freeze to death while they were at it."

"Humphrey Bogart would have dug up half a dozen witnesses by now and still had time to screw Mary Astor," Bobby said in disgust.

"And keep the fat man from killing him," Kate said sadly, "and the downtown dicks from arresting him, and keep the black bird for himself."

Jack heaved a deep, mournful sigh, probably over the unattainable Mary Astor.

The fire crackled in the fireplace and the thin arctic sun sent nearly horizontal beams in through Bobby's enormous windows. The reflection off the snow outside was painful to look at for long. Bobby rolled over and pulled the sheers to block it out.

Kate said to Jack, "Let's take a ride on up to Park Headquarters."

"Why? Gamble's already been up there. Everything he got is in the file."

She gave him an old-fashioned look. "The way Miller's call to his daddy was? I want to talk to the people who worked with Miller myself."

"Is there enough snow?"

"Of course there's enough snow, there was enough snow yesterday to—" She stopped and looked at him in sudden realization. To get to Park Headquarters would require another trip across Lost Chance Creek. "You don't have to come," she said gently. "And I'll come straight back here, I promise." Jack said nothing. "You hired me to do this job for you, Jack. And you're right, there probably isn't any reason for me to go. I've just got this itch, you know, like I'm staring right at something, like I'm bumping into the same thing over and over again, but I just can't—" She broke off and shook her head in frustration. "I'm going up there."

Jack set his jaw and reached for his boots. "You go, I go."

"No, really, Jack," she started to say.

"No, really, Kate," he mocked her. "The shrink said the more I faced up to it, the easier it'd get."

She looked at him, at the strained look around his eyes and the sweat already popping out on his forehead, and her heart melted. "We could fly in."

He looked at her, and the sweat on his brow was sucked back into his pores like magic. "I forgot they had a strip up there. How long is it?"

"Greg takes his Tri-Pacer in there all the time. I think it's about a thousand feet. Is that long enough?"

Jack's grin was wide and relieved and she had her answer. "Not that I can't cross that goddam bridge," he added, in case there was any doubt. "I just have to do it my own way."

"Of course," Kate murmured without the trace of a smile.

Bobby looked from one to the other and said, "Please don't bother to explain yourselves on my account. We mushrooms are used to being kept in the dark and fed shit three times a day. No, really," he added as they reached for parkas and snowsuits and headed for the door, "we like it." He was shouting variations on this original theme from his open doorway as Kate and Jack went off on the Super Jag, Mutt barking an indignant accompaniment next to him. Mutt didn't like being left behind. Bobby didn't like being left in the dark.

• • •

Park Headquarters was in the geographical center of the Park, on a natural plateau where the foothills left off and the mountains began. The gravel airstrip ran down its exact center, as if the people who had cleared and surfaced it were afraid that if they worked too close to either edge they might fall off the world. The plateau stood at a crossroads of sorts, between plain and mountain, between river and glacier, between civilization, such as it was, and wilderness, or what was left of it.

Jack side-slipped down to a three-point landing and rolled out to a stop thirty feet from the group of buildings clustered around the end of the runway. "Not bad," Kate had to admit. Jack's grin was smug. They climbed out and headed for the large building at the center of the cluster and went inside.

"Hey, Dan," Kate said, stretching out her hand with a warm smile. "Working hard or hardly working?"

He snorted, a tall man with a freckled face, bushy orange-red hair and twinkling blue eyes that could have charmed the British out of Northern Ireland. Kate had seen plenty of that twinkle when she met Dan for the first time; after a while he had discovered to his astonishment that she really didn't want to play anything but pinochle with him. He discovered to his further astonishment that, if he worked at it, he could be just friends with a woman. For a while he worried that the cold Alaskan air was sapping his virility, but one of Kate's aunts and two of her cousins dispelled that notion to everyone's complete satisfaction, and he relaxed and began to enjoy their relationship. "Hell, Kate," he said now, "between the squatters and the miners and the trappers and the hunters—"

"Okay, okay, Danny boy, enough whining. You'd stab anyone who tried to take this job away from you and you know it."

Dan propped his feet up on his desk and leaned back with

his hands linked behind his head. "I reckon you're here about Miller."

"I reckon you're right," Kate mimicked him, propping up her own feet. "Dan O'Brian, meet Jack Morgan. Jack's head of the D.A.'s investigative office, Dan."

Dan grinned at Jack. "Miller's daddy been after you?"

"He's been after the FBI, who've been after me."

"Yeah. They were up here, too." Dan shook his head. "I liked that kid, I really did. Lot of enthusiasm, lot of smarts, but he did wave his daddy like a flag. It could get tiring."

"Tiring enough for you to pull his plug?" Jack said hopefully.

Dan leaned back his head and laughed. "Sometimes, I admit, I'd liked to have strangled the sanctimonious little shit," he said. "And sometimes I'd have had to stand in line to do it. But I didn't. Neither did anybody else up here on the Step."

"You familiar with what he did the last day he was seen?"

"Shit, who isn't? Since Kate started sniffing around you can't work up a decent conversation on the CB without dragging Miller into it." He turned a bright, inquiring gaze on Kate.

"Danny boy," Kate said sadly, "we've got zilch. Every lead we've had has gone right down the toilet." She nodded at Jack. "When Miller disappeared Jack sent Ken Dahl in to look for him. Now he's missing, too."

Danny pursed his lips together in a silent whistle. "Blond, blue-eyed?"

"That's the guy. He come up here?"

Danny said blandly, "Yeah, he made it this far. I didn't know him from Adam, but I recognized him right away from the description Bernie gave me."

Caught off guard, Kate said, "How?"

"He had his mouth open." Kate reddened and Danny grinned. "What do you want to know, Kate? I told everything I knew to the feds when the FBI rode up on their white horse."

Kate was silent for a moment. "Tell me about him. Miller."

Dan looked at her, and drawled, "He was twenty-three. Short. Skinny. More energy than a nuclear power plant. More enthusiasm than a bull moose in rut. Talked all the time about My Father The Congressman."

"What did you have him doing?"

"Let's see, he got here early last spring, just after you nailed Sandy. Nice work, that, by the way. Poaching's down by more than half in the Park this winter from last. Lot less drunks waving their rifles around." Kate hoped Dan wouldn't be climbing down into Lost Chance Creek anytime soon. "Anyway, Miller. Last spring Mac Devlin was politicking to start work on the Carmack, so I sent Miller down there to check on the operation. Gave him the go-ahead to shut it down if Devlin was stepping out of line, which I and everyone else knew he was. Miller naturally found out, too, and he did shut him down."

Dan grinned. "So then Miller appointed himself guardian angel of every stream in the Park that had been frightened by the sight of a gold pan. He spent most of his time after that poking around mining and sledging operations, checking permits and runoff and seeing if the summer miners were packing out what trash they packed in. Hell, it needed doing, so I let him do it."

"How did he get along with people in the Park? People who lived here, I mean. Other than Mac."

"He didn't. Like I said, he'd been poking around the mines. It turned out he'd taken a mineralogy course in college. He

147

got his daddy to send him this little hammer, and he started taking samples out of every abandoned mine shaft he poked his head down." Dan shrugged. "You know how it is. Those old homesteaders aren't going to mine it themselves, but they're damned if they're going to let anyone else move in on them, either."

"Anybody in particular complain?"

"Nah, that's the funny thing. They'd stumble over him on their property and be breathing tar and feathers. Then he'd start talking to them about this vision he had of the mines opened up and operated by the government, which would use the profits to develop the Park for tourism. That boy was an Outsider from the word go and a king-size pain in the ass, but he had an idea that he believed in." Dan grinned at them. "And my, could he talk. That tongue of his was pure silver and jointed at both ends. Put him and Billy Graham in the same room and lock the door on them and my money'd be on Billy Graham coming out a born-again greenie. Yeah," Dan said, stretching, "Miller turned the tide on more than a few homesteads that I know of, and he crossed up Mac again and again, the last time over the Nabesna. But like I said, it needed doing. Devlin's needed somebody sitting on him since the first day he slunk back into the Park."

"The perfect ranger," Kate suggested.

"Well now, I wouldn't go that far." Dan scratched his belly and confessed, "I do admit I was glad Miller was mostly out in the field, because when he came up to Headquarters he always had a better idea how to run things."

"What things?"

"Anything," Dan said ruefully, and Kate and Jack laughed. "Yeah, it was funny at first, but when he started telling rangers who had been in the business twenty years how to clean out deadfall and counsel campers and ride herd on hunters, he was begging to get himself pushed off the Step." Dan shook his head, smiling at the memory. "He could wear you out."

"You liked Miller, too," Kate accused.

"What do you mean, 'too'?" Dan said, a little defensively.

"Bernie, Bobby, now you. All the people I'd expect to have hated the kid's guts. When you talk about him, you all get that same funny expression on your faces and that same funny tone in your voices, like you couldn't decide between sending him naked into a swamp full of mosquitoes or adopting him for a son and heir."

Dan shrugged uncomfortably. "Yeah. Well."

"What did you tell Ken Dahl when he showed up?"

Dan scratched his head. "Same thing I just told you."

"Anything else?"

"No. Wait a minute," Dan said. "We kept a copy of the transcript of the testimony in front of the House sub-committee. He wanted to see it, so I let him read it."

Kate exchanged a glance with Jack, who said, "Could we have a copy?"

"Sure." Dan rummaged around in an overflowing file cabinet for some twenty minutes, cursing beneath his breath all the while. Eventually, with an air of triumph Kate considered too mild in relation to the task accomplished, he produced a folder shedding sheets of paper like a fish shedding scales. "George!"

George, a thin young man with an enormous nose, a handlebar mustache and bare feet, stuck his head in the door and inquired in a serene voice, "You bellowed, your eminence?"

"Is that Xerox machine working today?"

"It's the only machine out here that is."

"Could you make a copy of this file for me?"

"Sure, but it's your fault if the paper jams."

"Live dangerously. Risk it." George left and Dan said, "Can I hitch a ride back to town with you? I got a girl in Niniltna I want to see."

"When don't you?" Kate said absently. She was frowning at her crossed ankles. Dan exchanged a quizzical glance with Jack, who shrugged. They waited.

Kate became aware of the silence that had fallen in the room and uncrossed her ankles. "No," she said, rising to her feet. "No, you can't hitch a ride with us. I'm sorry, Dan, but we're not going back to Niniltna just yet."

Jack shot her a quick look, but said nothing.

Dan shrugged and grinned. "I'll get on the CB and get her to come up here."

"Who is it this time?" Kate said.

"A gentleman never kisses and tells," Dan said virtuously, and pretended offense when Jack laughed at him.

● ● ●

Jack followed Kate outside to the airstrip, tucking the bulky file in his parka pocket. She stood next to the Cessna in silence without moving, her eyes troubled. At last Jack said, "Where are we going?"

She stood, irresolute, not replying. Jack nudged her and repeated the question.

Her chin lifted. He heard her take a deep breath and she turned and said, "Have you got enough gas to get us to Anchorage?"

"You want to go to town now?"

"Yes."

"From here?"

"Yes."

He looked at her. "We've got enough gas. Why do you want to go to town?"

"I want to bail Chick out of jail."

Her answer rocked him back a little. "Chick who?" he said cautiously.

"Chick Noyukpuk." Jack's expression remained blank and Kate said, "The Billiken Bullet." Still no response, and Kate said with asperity, "It is inconceivable to me that you have lived for twenty-two years in this state and you still don't know who the Billiken Bullet is."

"Who is he?" Jack said meekly.

Kate gave a martyred sigh. "He's Mandy's roomie." She looked at him and added, "Mandy? Next door to Abel? You know—"

"The lady with more dogs than James Thurber," he interrupted. "I remember now, the little guy with no front teeth. They mush dogs."

Kate closed her eyes for a moment. "Yes," she said, opening them. "They mush dogs. And they live together."

"Oh." Jack thought it over, and added, "When he's not in jail, you mean."

"When Chick's not in jail," Kate agreed.

"And you want to bail him out?"

"Yes."

"What's he in for?"

Kate gestured vaguely. "The usual. Drunk and disorderly. Disturbing the peace. Assaulting a police officer. Resisting arrest."

Jack took a deep breath, and let it out slowly. "Oh. That usual. Mind telling me why we're bailing him out?" Kate opened her mouth, and then closed it again. "No, huh?"

"It's just a hunch," she muttered, more to herself than to him.

"Okay," he said simply. "Let's go."

CHAPTER 9

"I DIDN'T TAKE the damn thing," Chick said. "I told that damn trooper in Anchorage, and I told that damn judge— Did you hear what she said to me?"

"Who said?"

"That judge who sentenced me," Chick said, sitting up straight on Bobby's couch and looking indignant.

They had made the trip to Anchorage and back in record time, and all Kate saw of town was Fifth Avenue on the way to the Cook Inlet Pre-Trial Facility, Third Avenue on the way to the courthouse, and Sixth Avenue on the way back to Merrill Field, all of them glittering red and green with Christmas decorations. It was late in the afternoon when they took off for the return trip, and the sun had long since set. Strobes from the tops of the Arco and BP towers and exhaust from the traffic made the streets look like something out of *Faust*. She was inexpressibly relieved when they were airborne and outbound. Sitting next to her, she knew Jack had felt the tension build on the way into town and ebb on the way out, and she was grateful that he knew enough to remain silent.

Chick Noyukpuk, oblivious to any emotional trauma experienced by anyone not himself, slept his way home curled up in a blanket in the backseat. Now he was wide awake, drinking coffee laced with Wild Turkey and watching hungrily as Bobby barbecued moose steaks on the fireplace grill.

"What did the judge say?" Jack said, resigned to playing straight man.

"She said I was a convicted felon and couldn't vote no more."

"Oh," Jack said. He raised an eyebrow in Kate's direction.

"Have you ever voted?" she asked Chick.

"No," Chick said belligerently, "but that don't mean I don't want to. You just wait till the next election, I'll vote, by God I will." He pushed his jaw out. There was a moment of silence. "When's the next election?" he said.

"It'll be a while," Jack said in a soothing voice.

"But I still didn't steal that goddam snow machine," Chick said, uncharacteristically reverting to his original complaint. He saw Kate's skepticism and raised his voice. "I didn't, Kate. On top of knowing I'd be back in the guest cabin when I got home if I did steal the damn thing, have you ever known me to pass up a ride on a Snowcat?" She said nothing, and he demanded, "Well?"

"No," Kate said slowly, "no, I haven't."

"Who says there was one?" Bobby muttered to Jack, but the big man was watching Kate and didn't respond.

A minute passed, and another. A third went the same way and Bobby couldn't stand it. "Is this the little gray cells' part?" he begged. "Huh, is it, is it?"

"Shut up," Kate said curtly, without looking at him. "I'm thinking."

"Oh well, pardon me all to hell, she's thinking," Bobby told Jack. He forked the steaks off the grill in offended silence and handed brimming plates around.

Chick sniffed his dinner and closed his eyes in ecstasy. "Real food! Now I know I'm home."

Kate looked down at the moose steak on her plate, a little

charred and sizzling still from the grill. She cut a piece and lifted it halfway to her mouth, and paused, looking at the steaming, pink meat oozing juices. She dropped her fork back on her plate and pushed it away.

"What's the matter?" Bobby asked. "Something wrong with your steak?"

"No."

Bobby picked up her plate and inspected the cut of meat. "I can grill up another if you—"

"No, Bobby, thanks anyway. I'm not really that hungry."

"Never known you to turn down one of my steaks before," Bobby said, hurt. The men set to without further conversation, cleaning their plates. Bobby, still offended or pretending to be, whisked the debris into the kitchen and badgered Chick into washing the dishes, watching with such a merciless eye that Chick, unnerved, broke two plates.

Kate dug the minutes of October's subcommittee hearing out of Jack's parka pocket and settled into a corner of the couch to read. Jack watched her for a while. She didn't look up. She didn't look as if she remembered anyone else was in the room.

The three men gathered around the kitchen table and played cutthroat pinochle. Chick got a double run during the first game, a thousand aces during the second and shot the moon not once but twice during the third. Jack sighed and got out his wallet, again. Bobby, glowering, growled, "Goddam cardsharp."

Chick, abashed at beggaring the man who had just fed him the best dinner he'd had in two weeks, or perhaps apprehensive that the offer of a bed for the night might be revoked, offered to return it all, but Bobby wouldn't hear of it. "No, really," he said through his teeth, "if I went out playing pinochle any way but through the back door, it would feel unnatural. Ask Kate."

The three men turned to look at her. Kate had finished reading the minutes and was sitting, motionless, staring blindly into the fire. Her face was pale and so without expression Jack thought she might be asleep, until he saw that Mutt was sitting in front of her, staring into Kate's face with her yellow eyes wide and unblinking. As he watched, Mutt turned her head and looked at him and whined. It was a muted, anxious little whine, unlike anything he'd heard Mutt say before. A full-throated, head-back, moon-calling howl couldn't have brought him up out of his chair any faster.

He hesitated, and then with an elaborate show of casualness he strolled across the room to stand next to Mutt. "Finished reading?" he said, stooping to pick up the file folder.

She didn't answer. He tried again. "Find anything interesting?"

She said nothing.

"Kate? What is it?"

Kate stirred, and turned to look at Bobby. "Bobby, how cold has it been the last two weeks?"

Bobby, still smarting, said nastily, "Weather you want? Weather you got." He wheeled himself over to his place of business, mumbling to himself. He flipped through the weather charts, the figures of which he radioed in daily to Anchorage, and compared their figures with the data compiler he mailed in from Niniltna once a month. "What you want, winds, temp, what?"

"Temperature."

"Been below freezing since November 21, when this cold snap set in. Below average snowfall, zip in this case."

Kate listened without looking at him. Her continued lack of expression alarmed Jack, and he tossed the committee's minutes aside and sat down next to her. He put a tentative arm around her shoulders, and when she didn't shrug it away he was really alarmed. "Kate?"

A switch closed, a thread snapped, the other shoe dropped. Kate closed her eyes and folded her arms across her stomach and bent forward, hugging herself.

"Kate?" Jack said.

"What the hell?" Bobby said.

"What's going on?" Chick said, bewildered. "What's the matter with a cold spell? We have them all the time. It's hell on the dogs' feet, but it sure speeds up the races."

Mutt hopped up on the couch on Kate's other side and put her cold nose against Kate's cheek, whining anxiously.

Bobby wheeled his chair around smartly and sent it whizzing over in front of Kate. He said, gently for Bobby, "Woman, you look like you're about to make a call on the porcelain phone. Put your head down between your knees before you pass out." Kate pulled feebly at his hands, and he said, "Okay, then put your head down between my knees."

Kate's laugh was closer to hysteria than humor. Bobby looked at Jack with a worried expression.

Jack got up and went to stand next to the fireplace. His large frame was backlit by the flames and his shadow loomed large over the room. "You know what happened." His face was in shadow, his deep voice disembodied, unemotional, but nevertheless commanding a response.

Bobby shot him an angry glance, but Kate's answer forestalled him. "Yes," she said. Bobby had never heard his indomitable Kate sound so hopeless, not even when she had told him she would never sing again. "I think I do."

Again that depersonalized demand. "Where's the kid?"

Again the despairing answer. "Dead."

157

"And Ken?"

She looked up and met his hard blue gaze. "Dead."

There was silence. Chick reached stealthily for the bottle of Wild Turkey and refilled his glass.

Jack sat down heavily on the edge of the hearth and was transformed from demanding, authoritative giant to weary, unhappy mortal. "Well, hell, Kate," he said, rubbing his eyes. "Both of them?"

"I think so." There was silence, and then she said, "And I think I know where they are."

"And who put them there?"

She was silent a long time. When she spoke, it was one single, rough syllable. "Yes."

He shoved his hands in his pockets and crossed his feet at the ankles. Unseen by them, his hands clenched into fists. "All right, Kate," he said, his words even. "Run it down for me."

When she finished speaking, Bobby said flatly, "You're nuts," and Chick, whom they had all forgotten was there, laughed out loud.

Jack, his face a mask, said curtly, "And Ken?"

Kate sat up, moving like an old woman, and rose to her feet. She walked across to the windows and looked out. The scene outside could have been painted by Sydney Lawrence, all plump white snowdrifts, thickly clustered scrub spruce, a waning white moon balanced on the edge of the Quilaks as it made ready to slip out of the sky. Mutt padded after her and squatted at her feet, her nose lifted, yellow gaze fixed unwaveringly on Kate's face. "Ken was a good investigator," she said at last. Her lips compressed into a thin, bitter smile. "Better than me."

"And?" For all his fatigue, Jack was inexorable.

Kate shook her head. "What I couldn't see at first because

158

I was too close to it, was what he saw in a straight line, simple cause and effect. I think it killed him."

Her words trailed away into shadow and silence. There was a long pause. A log split, crackled and hissed in the fireplace.

Jack stirred. "So we go out there tomorrow? Confront him?"

She shook her head. "The bodies first. We have to be sure." She looked at Jack, her brown eyes blind with a kind of anguish. He had to fight not to reach out to her. "I'll need your help."

• • •

She climbed on her Super Jag the next morning. Mutt hopped up behind her and Jack followed on Bobby's Polaris. No one said much of anything, and Bobby saw them off without heaping any more abuse on Kate's reconstruction of events. He remained skeptical, but worried with it, and took it out on his hapless and hung-over houseguest, shaking him awake and handing him a broom.

"Fall cleaning?" Chick said, befuddled and still not entirely sober. "It's almost Christmas."

"So I got a little behind," Bobby barked.

"Mandy's gonna kill me," Chick pleaded, "I've gotta get home."

"After the sweeping," Bobby said, and a miserable but obedient Chick went to work with the broom.

• • •

For eight sleepless hours Kate had replayed the evidence in her head, trying to find a way around it, over it, away from it,

159

trying to make it mean anything but what she knew in her heart to be the exact, unvarnished truth. The night before she lay on one section of Bobby's couch and Jack lay on another, Chick snoring between them, wrapped up in a sleeping bag on the floor. Each knew the other was awake, but they did not speak once through all the long hours of the night, while the fire popped and hissed on the hearth, when a wolf howled far away, as the moon crept from the sky.

However much she tried, she had not been able to hold back the morning. She took her time on the trail, covering each of the thirty miles from Bobby's homestead deliberately, taking time to appreciate the slowly lightening sky, the graceful arcs of tree limbs bowed beneath glittering frost, the ponderous dignity of a cow moose in snow up to her shoulders, munching on an alder. The cold of the morning seemed to seep ever more deeply into her bones, until she felt as numb on the outside as she did on the inside. She was grateful for it, although she did stop once to check her hands and feet to make sure. Every digit was warm and vital and vibrant. Everything Mark Miller and Kenneth Dahl were not. Behind her she could hear the steady purr of Jack on the Polaris, but she never once turned around to look.

Halfway to their destination they came across a yearling moose who had broken his left foreleg jumping from a high bank. He was alive, but only just, and he barely blinked when Kate pulled up and reached for her rifle. Not so the wolverine gnawing on the calf's broken leg, who snarled and feinted a lunge at them. Mutt growled deep in her throat from her perch behind Kate.

"Quiet, girl," Kate said. She put one bullet between the yearling's eyes and let another dust snow into the wolverine's face. He snarled again but stayed where he was.

160

"Aren't you going to shoot him?" Jack said from behind her. "I thought you hated wolverines."

"I do."

"Well?"

She watched the wolverine turn a contemptuous back to them and tear into the dead yearling's throat. She did not flinch at the steaming gush of blood that followed to stain the white snow and the wolverine's thick pelt and the young moose's brown hide. "First come, first served." And then she said, "He's only protecting what's his." She put the Jag in gear and rolled off.

She circled around Mandy's homestead, following what she remembered to be the rough track left by the surveyors marking the property line between Abel's homestead and Mandy's lodge. The ice over Silver Bottom Creek was frozen hard, the snow on either side equally so. The day was clear and calm. They saw no one. After a while Kate found the clearing that marked the start of the well-trodden trail that led up to the high cliffs, cliffs that in places towered hundreds of feet over the Kanuyaq River. Abel was always going up to the Lost Wife to chip away at some vein or other, looking without any urgency for the streak that would lead him to El Dorado. She took her thumb off the throttle and waited for Jack to catch up to her.

"This the way?" he said, peeling his ice-encrusted muffler away from his beard so he could speak clearly.

She nodded without turning and gunned the Jag up the trail.

It took them fifteen minutes to reach the mine, fifteen minutes of steep, narrow trail hemmed in on both sides with fir and birch. It climbed steadily, switching back and forth. Kate had to lean sharply into each turn to get the Jag safely around the corners, and her shoulders were aching by the time she was finally able to pull up. Her hands were cramped on the controls; it took a few fumbles to shut down the engine. Jack slid to a halt next to her and did the same, and except for Mutt's panting breaths peace of a sort broke out.

It was a larger clearing than the one at the foot of the trail, neatly shoveled and well packed. A layer of snow hid the pile of railroad ties ripped up by Abel's father when the Kanuyaq River & Northern Railroad stopped running in 1938. Another layer covered the heap of tailings raised up from the mine. Hemlocks clustered thickly at the edge of a well-defined circle, and behind them the foothills rose rapidly into the Quilak Mountains, blue-white and haughty in the pale, thin light of morning.

"The forest primeval," Jack said, and shivered. "Jesus, it's cold."

Kate got off her machine and walked toward the depression lying up against the base of the cliff. The entrance to the Lost Wife was the size of a double door, framed in railroad ties and set into the face of a short, crumbling wall of rock and gravel. A set of parallel metal tracks led inside. A small cart on metal wheels stood just outside, filled with broken rocks and debris.

Kate pulled the cart back. Inside the mine's entrance a wide hole gaped, opening straight down into the ground. It looked black and bottomless.

"How do we get down?" Jack said from behind her.

"There's a dumbwaiter kind of gadget."

Jack swallowed. "How deep is that damn thing, anyway?" he asked in a gruff voice.

"It's sunk about a hundred and fifty feet, the last time we measured," she said. "There are tunnels leading off from three or four different levels."

162

"Oh."

She looked at him. "You don't have to go," she said. "The dumbwaiter can take only one of us at a time, anyway, and I weigh less. And I've been down it before." She saw shame and relief wash over his face in equal parts. "Don't," she said, laying one mittened hand on his arm.

He looked at her and she saw some of the shame recede. She squeezed his arm and let go. "I'm going to need a flashlight. Abel disconnects the generator from the mine in September so all the power will go to the homestead during the winter."

She turned toward the entrance and saw Mutt's ears go up and the dog's head swivel toward the woods, and with an intuition she was never able to account for afterward she threw herself sideways, knocking Jack down a split second before they heard the crack of a rifle and a bullet's thud into the timber holding up the roof of the mine. There was a shower of ice shards from the branches of trees clinging to the cliff above the entrance of the mine. Instinctively Kate rolled for cover, into the mine, away from the downpour, and slid over the edge of the open shaft.

For one grateful moment she felt the solid presence of the dumbwaiter platform beneath her, before it gave way in little jerks and bounces as the tackle slid over a rope spliced with many repairs. "Jack!" she yelled. "Help!" For a terrifying second a new section of rope ran freely through the tackle and it felt as if the bottom had dropped out of her universe. Her head snapped up to see the open square of light at the top of the shaft receding rapidly, and she screamed, "Jack! Grab the rope!"

There was no answer. Kate came alive and beat the air wildly, scrabbled at the walls of the shaft, until by some miracle one of her flailing hands swatted the loose line. She grabbed for it and her progress halted abruptly, jarring her teeth. For a moment she was absolutely still.

The slick fabric of her gloves slid down the rope one inch, another.

Moving very, very slowly, lifting one finger at a time from the rope, she ditched the gloves and wound first one hand and then the other around her slender lifeline.

The dumbwaiter creaked a little in protest, and stopped sliding.

She closed her eyes and leaned her forehead against knotted knuckles. Her breathing sounded like a steam engine in her ears. She tried to bring it under control. Her legs and lower body still lay on top of the dumbwaiter. The muscles in her arms contorted painfully as she tried to put all her weight on the rope.

"Son of a bitch," she said out loud. "I just might talk my way out of this after all."

Her head swam in dizzy relief and, teeth clenched, she waited for the dizziness to pass. She became aware of Mutt barking hysterically from the top of the shaft, but no other sound. She gathered all her strength. "Jack!" she yelled. He didn't answer. "Jack!" she yelled again. "Damn you if you picked now to get shot I'll *kill* you!" She craned her head, straining to see up the shaft, the rope pressing into her cheek.

His head was suddenly silhouetted next to Mutt's against the light at the top of the shaft. He had her flashlight in his hand, and he switched it on and played it over the inside of the shaft. It was a long, long way down before he found Kate dangling at the end of her rope, her white face raised to his, her eyes staring up at him. "Oh God," he said. Mutt whined anxiously next to him.

"Jack," she said hoarsely, "can you hear me?"

"Yes," he said, the struggle for control obvious in his voice. "Yes, I can hear you."

"Okay. Something's wrong with the dumbwaiter, the rope's broke or something. Can you grab the safety?"

"The what?"

"The safety—the rope tied off to the cleat next to the entrance."

"Oh God," he said again, the light of the flash playing over her, and she heard him swallow.

Suddenly she realized what was wrong with him. "Jack!"

"Okay, honey, I'm on it. Just hang on, sweetheart."

His head disappeared. So did the light, and Kate was plunged once more into darkness. She controlled a wave of hysteria and, sweating with the strain, lifted herself to put a little slack in the rope and take another turn of it around her lower wrist.

She waited. Seconds stretched into hours, minutes into days. Beads of sweat ran into her eyes and off her nose and chin. The dumbwaiter quivered beneath her, reminding her of a lead dog in a race before the starting gun was fired.

Jack's head reappeared and with it the infinitely welcome beam of the flashlight. "Okay, I've got the end of the rope on belay around a tree. I'm going to take it off the cleat now, so you're going to drop a little."

"Jack?" she said, her voice coming from a long distance.

"What?"

"Jack?" she said again.

"It's okay, honey," he said. "I'll leave the flashlight this time, I had to use it to find the cleat before. Just hang on."

His head disappeared again. She waited, her eyes closed, the muscles in her arms trembling. The rope jerked between her hands and loosened, and again the bottom fell out of her world. She couldn't stifle the scream that bubbled to her lips.

The dumbwaiter fell again and her with it. It slammed to an abrupt stop four or five feet farther down the shaft. Sharp pain clawed at her wrists, and she cried out. She slipped across the top of the tiny platform and thudded into the opposite wall of the shaft. Rocks loosened and fell. A long time later she heard them hit bottom. Her wrists, her entire arms were numb. After a moment she felt a warm, dripping moisture where the rope was wound.

"Kate?" Jack yelled. "Kate?"

She couldn't speak. He fumbled with the flashlight so that the beam was trained at her. Her head was leaning against her forearms, and he couldn't see her face. "Kate, answer me. You've got to help me with your feet when I start hauling on this rope. Kate, say something, talk to me!"

"All right," she said in a faint voice. "I heard you."

He sagged against the shaft opening. "Thank God. Did you hear what I said about helping me?"

"Yes," she muttered.

"What?"

"Yes, I heard you."

Jack stared down, down, down the shaft, and the distance finally caught up with him. "Oh God, I'm going to puke," he groaned.

"Not now!" Kate shouted, galvanized. "Pull, goddam you!"

But there was a choking and burping sound above her. Kate jerked back but a cascade of warm, gloppy fluid grazed her cheek and spilled down over her parka front anyway.

It was possible that if Jack had worked it out a year in advance he could not have done anything to take Kate's mind more thoroughly off her present situation. She forgot that she

166

was dangling precariously over a mine shaft a hundred and fifty feet deep. She forgot that someone had shot at her moments before. She forgot that she needed every ounce of strength and courage just to keep herself alive. She cursed Jack Morgan. She called the legitimacy of his birth into question, swore to kill him if she ever got out of this mine alive, and promised fervently if she died to kill him anyway. She was loud, fluent and impassioned. Bobby would have been proud of her. Not for nothing was Kate Shugak Abel Inthout's foster daughter.

"Feel better now, you prick?" she yelled finally.

Jack cleared his throat and, sounding apologetic, called down to her, "I do, actually. You got the safety?"

She fumbled among the various ropes attached to the block. "Give it a tug. Okay, got it." Carefully, cautiously, she unwrapped her end from its cleat on the dumbwaiter platform. The line felt smooth and slender and fragile between her burning palms, but she was going to have to trust it—there was no other way out for her. She pulled herself up with her arms, lifting her body clear of the dumbwaiter. She wound one foot in the now dangling end of the safety. Cautiously she increased her weight on that foot. The line slid at first, then held. She breathed again.

All her weight was now on the safety. She waited for the dumbwaiter to crash down to the bottom of the shaft. It dropped a foot, creaking ominously.

"Kate?"

The flashlight blinded her. "I'm on the safety. Start pulling."

"Hang on." His head disappeared again.

"Like I had a choice," she muttered to herself. She tried to get some kind of purchase on the wall of the shaft with her free boot.

His voice came to her as from a great distance. "Ready?"

"Of course I'm ready, you—"

"Okay, here goes!"

She felt the rope bite again into the skin of her hands, and braced her free leg. Painfully she inched her way up the wall of the shaft, scrabbling with her foot to take advantage of every depression in the sheer face, every nubbin of rock, every marginally rough spot. The rope stripped her wrists of any remaining skin; her arms and back screamed under the strain. It seemed like forever, but was actually less than three minutes before she tumbled out of the mouth of the shaft.

She caught a confused glimpse of Mutt with the far end of the safety gripped between bared teeth before Jack dropped the rope and pounced on her. Fists knotted in her parka, he hauled her away from the mouth of the mineshaft, down the tracks, out of the entrance of the Lost Wife Mine and twenty feet down the trail before she managed to get him stopped.

"Jack! Jack! Jack, it's all right. I'm okay, I'm safe. Stop now. Stop." Mutt trotted next to them, uttering short, distressed barks.

Jack slowed down finally, and stopped. He gazed down at her, haggard and exhausted, and no one had ever looked that good to her before in all her thirty years of living. "I'm okay," she repeated. "Take it easy. I'm all right now. We're both all right."

She tugged at his arm. He crumpled next to her, falling to his knees and dropping his head on her shoulder. His arms came around to hold her so tightly she couldn't breathe. Mutt touched her cold nose to Kate's cheek and whined. Kate put her other arm around her dog. "Hush now," she told them both, hugging as much of them as she could and rocking back and forth. "Hush now. Everything's all right now."

They stayed that way for a long time, until the chill of the snow-covered ground penetrated her snowsuit and she began to shiver. Jack felt her tremble and pulled away to look into her face. "Kate," he said, tugging off a mitten and cupping her cheek in one large palm. "Oh, Kate." He leaned forward and touched her lips with his and rested his forehead against hers. "Oh, Kate."

"I'm hungry," she said. "I don't know why, but I'm starving. Could you find something for us to eat?"

He struggled wearily to his feet and fetched the first aid kit from the Polaris. He cleaned and bandaged her wrists and palms and pulled her sleeves back down. He got the canteen from the Jag and she drank from it thirstily. The three of them demolished two packages of beef jerky, made serious inroads on a ziploc bag full of Bobby's homemade trail mix and shared a Hershey bar for dessert.

"I'll go down this time," Jack announced firmly as he cleared up the debris from their meal.

Cleaning her face and the front of her snowsuit with handfuls of snow, Kate looked over at the entrance to the Lost Wife. He watched her. "I'm going and that's that," he said, his voice raising. "There's a pulley hanging over the shaft. I'll rig up a sling with the main line off the dumbwaiter and lower myself down."

"We don't have to go down now," she said, shifting her gaze to his face. "Before we weren't sure."

He was silent for a moment. "And now we are?"

She dropped her head and wished she could cry. "I am."

• • •

The homestead had not changed in three days. There had been no snow here, either, and the hard-packed surface around the buildings showed little difference between visitors who had come and gone six weeks ago, two weeks ago or two days ago. Kate walked slowly, with Mutt trotting in front of her. After strenuous protests, Jack had reluctantly agreed to remain at the top of the trail.

Abel was waiting for her on his doorstep with a rough hug and a mug of coffee. She accepted both and followed him inside, where her knees were shaking so that she had to lean up against the kitchen counter to steady herself. She couldn't look at him. She let her eyes wander around the room. They stopped at the coatrack. "You've already been out this morning, Abel."

He looked at her, a trace of uneasiness in the fierce, faded blue eyes, a trace, almost, of fear. She'd never seen such an expression on his face before, and it hurt her. For the first time she saw, or allowed herself to see, the age spots on the backs of his gnarled hands, the imperceptible tremor in the way he held his head, the slight stoop of his shoulders. Abel had looked older than God for the last thirty years, that was nothing new, but he had never seemed vulnerable until now. "How'd you know that, girl?"

She pointed. "Snow melting off your boots."

"Oh." They stared at his boots together. Abel drew himself up and smiled at her. "Want some lunch, girl?"

"No, Abel," she said. Her body stopped trembling and all at once she felt unnaturally calm. "I can't stay. I told you, I'm looking for someone. I've got to keep looking for them until I find them."

He snorted. His cheeks were ruddy with the cold and his thinning hair was mussed. "Some damn park ranger and a guy poking his nose in where it didn't belong. Not much loss if you never find them, seems to me."

Kate said steadily, "I've just come from your daddy's old silver mine, Abel."

He kept his head down, unwilling or unable to look at her. "Now why would you want to go messing around up there?" he said at last.

"Because I thought I'd find two bodies at the bottom of the shaft, Abel," she said. She met the old man's fierce blue gaze without flinching. "One belongs to a park ranger named Mark Miller. The other belongs to an investigator attached to the Anchorage District Attorney's Office who came up here looking for him, named Kenneth Dahl."

The old man tried to laugh. "Dead folks on my property that I don't know about! Girl, I think you worked for them ambulance chasers in town for too long; you're seeing bodies everywhere."

"Oh, I think you know about them, Abel. I think you put them there."

Abel exploded, his face turning a deep, congested red. "What! Why, what's got into you, girl, I never did no such—"

Kate went on as if he hadn't interrupted her, her voice a dead, husky monotone. "You had a run-in with Miller at the committee hearing in Niniltna. He wanted to make the Park a park; you want to keep it your own private homestead. He wanted to let people in; you want to keep them out. I read your testimony, Abel. You were angry, maybe as angry as you've ever been, and that's pretty angry."

Her voice broke. She steadied it and went on, dry-eyed. "I figure Miller came up here, maybe that night, maybe even the next morning, early, driving his Land Cruiser, to argue with you some more. He knew your family has a lot of clout in

Juneau. He probably wanted to try to swing you around to his side, help out his holy cause. You argued." She looked at him, trying to smile. "You've got a temper, Abel. Maybe he was so young and enthusiastic that you knew he was going to win just by outlasting you, or maybe he was just too much of an Outsider for you to stomach, or maybe you were afraid his congressman father pulled too much weight and you'd lose it all. Maybe all those things. At any rate, he made you mad, and—"

"I didn't mean to do it," the old man interrupted her suddenly, his body slumping. For a moment Kate thought he was going to fall where he stood, and she put out a steadying hand. "He was standing right where you are, drinking my coffee and eating my Twinkies and spouting all that crap about public access, and how federal lands belonged to all the people and not just the ones who wanted to keep their own private...fiefdoms, I think he called them. Why couldn't he talk plain English while he was at it?"

Abel shook his head like a bear trying to shake off a persistent bee. "I was so damn mad I don't remember exactly what he said. I had the coffeepot in my hand, and I was talking with it, you know how I do. He must have thought I was going to clobber him with it because the next thing I know, he's backing up and tripping over a chair and falling down and banging himself on the oven door. I always keep it open in the winter, Kate, you know that. He caught his head right on the corner. He was dead before I touched him. It was an accident, Kate. That damn oven door and his own foolishness was what killed him. I could see somebody already'd been banging on him, his face was all busted up. He must have been feeling kinda woozy already, and lost his balance. It was an accident," he repeated. "Just a damn fool accident, that's all."

Kate set her coffee down and stepped away from the stove. "If it was an accident, why didn't you tell Dan O'Brian, or Chopper Jim?"

His eyes slid away. "Oh hell, girl. After we'd gone at it bare-knuckled at that hearing, do you think anybody would believe me when I told them the kid tripped over his own feet?"

"You could have tried."

"Well, I didn't," Abel said, almost sulky.

She waited, and when he said nothing else she continued. "The next morning you used the Land Cruiser to haul Miller's body up to the Lost Wife. Then you loaded your sled and the dogs into the back and drove to the Roadhouse before Bernie was up. You hitched up the dogs and went down the road a little or maybe into the woods, and waited for the bar to open so Bernie could see you mush up for your weekly shot of bourbon."

Her rough voice was dispassionate. Kate was beyond hurling accusations. She waited, but he said nothing. She had to ask the question she had been dreading. "What about Kenneth Dahl?"

Abel's eyes narrowed. He looked feral, even savage. "I caught him up to the Lost Wife two weeks ago and he says he wants to go down her. I tell him no and he says he's going down her anyway. What call's he got trespassing on my property, tell me that! So I pull down on him with the Winchester."

"And you missed, and he ran," Kate said. "So you kept shooting."

"Yeah," Abel said, surprised. "How'd you know?"

"Mandy heard you shooting. She said it sounded like a bunch of poachers. You got him after all, though, didn't you?"

Abel said nothing.

"I figure by the time you got him you were on Mandy's land and too tired to take him all the way back up the hill. So you snuck into the lodge and stole her new snow machine. You used it to drag Ken's body back here. You sacked it up in a game bag and hung it under the cache to freeze so it would be easier to get up to the mine. Then you took the snow machine out and wrecked it, so Mandy would think Chick had done it. Nice of Chick to go on a bender right about then, wasn't it? And then you came home. You're not young anymore, Abel. That was why Ken's body was still hanging beneath the cache when I came."

Abel said nothing.

"Oh, Abel," she said, closing her eyes. "I fought like hell not to believe it was you, but everywhere I looked, there you were. Testifying before the committee. Next door when Mandy's snow machine was stolen. At the Roadhouse the morning Miller's Toyota reappeared. I just couldn't get away from you."

"My pa was a Ninety-Niner, girl," he said. At his tone she opened her eyes and saw tears in his. "He left Nome and came up the Yukon and down the Kanuyaq and found this place and staked it for his own. Anna and I built on to the place and raised our family here. This place will be Abel Junior's someday. I gotta hold it for him, no matter what."

She said, and there was a great weariness in her voice, "To the extent of murder?"

"Oh hell, Kate," he said scornfully, "killing a park ranger in Alaska ain't the same thing as murder and you know it. They ain't much better than fish hawks, and your own father accounted for at least one of them. God knows," the old man said with a mixture of bewilderment and exhaustion, "God

174

knows that however many of them we run off ten more spring up in their place. They're like that goddam Greek thing you used to tell me about, the one where you cut off his head, two more grows in its place. Remember?"

"The Hydra," Kate said. Her voice broke. "Oh, Abel."

"Kate," the old man said, almost pitifully, and for Kate that was worse than all the rest. "Kate," he repeated, "we let them rangers come in here and make them surveys and put in them campgrounds and pretty soon we'll be up to our ass in Winnebagoes. And if that happens I might as well move to Anchorage and buy one of them trailers across from the Northway Mall and let the Cessnas from Merrill Field land on my head all day and police cars run their sirens around me all night. I can't let that happen." Kate was silent, and he said, begging her, "Tell me you understand what I'm saying, girl."

She said softly, "I can understand the ranger, Abel. I can even believe you when you say it was an accident. But Ken?"

"He found out! He came up here, nosing around, asking questions. When I found him poking into the Lost Wife..." Abel's voice trailed off and he was silent. Finally he said, pleading, "I knew you was shacking up with him, girl, but what else could I do?"

"When you followed me into Niniltna, it wasn't because you were afraid I might get hurt. It was because you were afraid of what I might find out. And then when you heard it was Martin who was shooting at us at the NorthCom shack, you figured that would be enough to convince me that Martin killed Miller and Dahl, so you came home. But just in case, you sabotaged the dumbwaiter, and stood guard." She raised her head and stared straight into his eyes. "And then you shot at me to make me fall."

"I been meaning to fix that dumbwaiter for weeks," Abel

said quickly, "and I wasn't trying to kill you, I was just warning you off, trying to scare you a little."

Kate almost laughed. "That's the second time this week someone's shot at me and not meant to kill me." She shook her head. "Maybe you and Martin should get together."

Abel stiffened. "It's so easy for you, Kate," he said, his old, thin voice rising. "The Native Claims Act gave you land and money, the Bureau of Indian Affairs paid your way to Anchorage when you were sick and took care of your medical bills when you got well, your father left you a home. I've had to work for everything I've got and then fight to keep it! Don't look down your nose at me for that!"

Kate looked at Abel, the man greatly responsible for the woman she was. She shook her head. "I am sick and tired of people telling me how easy I've had it. Emaa, Xenia, Martin, the rest of my family. Now you. None of you tried to take out a student loan and had the loan officer at the bank tell you you had to have a white cosigner. None of you had to sit in a history class and listen to the white Outside teacher tell you how the Aleuts spread their legs for Alexander Baranov. And none of you has ever had a welder from Tulsa, Oklahoma, call you a nigger. You're white in a white world, Abel, so don't talk to me about easy." Kate turned abruptly and went to the door.

"Where are you going, Kate?"

"To the village. To tell Billy Mike what I found out. So he can call Chopper Jim, and they can come up here and recover the bodies."

"No you ain't. Kate?"

She stepped through the door. She heard him moving behind her, heard him grunt when he got down his rifle, heard the sharp click of metal against metal. Next to her Mutt growled and tensed as if to leap.

"No, Mutt," Kate said in a cold, gentle voice. "Come."

"Kate, don't do it, I'm tellin' you."

The dog looked from Abel to Kate and back again. "Come," Kate repeated.

Dry-eyed, her spine straight, she took one step, another, a third. Mutt fell in next to her mistress, her puzzled yellow eyes lifted to Kate's, her plume of a tail curled over her back into a question mark.

"I'll shoot, Kate, I swear I will."

Kate stumbled, recovered, and walked on, her pulse drumming high up in her throat. If Abel actually was capable of killing her, she'd rather be dead anyway.

"A man's got a right, a duty to protect his home he's worked for for eighty years, Kate!"

Kate didn't look around. If, when it came, she didn't want to see it.

She was almost to the head of the trail when the shot echoed down off the indifferent shoulders of the Quilaks. Stumbling for the second time, almost falling, she caught herself against a tree trunk and waited for the pain to begin, for the warm, salty run of blood up into her mouth, the shock, followed by agonizing, debilitating pain. She knew what to expect. Leaning her forehead against the bark of the spruce, she braced herself and waited.

There was nothing, only the silent stillness of the forest, only the endless horizon of the sky. She understood, and the pain of her next inhalation hurt so much she wished she had been shot. Mutt looked up at her and whined anxiously.

"Kate!" Jack came crashing down the path, his face white. "Kate!" He grabbed her and for the second time that day ran anxious hands over her body. "I heard a shot! Are you all right? Are you hurt? Show me!"

Finding the words took a little time. "I'm all right," she said in a rusty voice.

His hands stilled. "I heard a shot," he repeated.

"Yes."

He looked behind her. "Where's Abel?"

"Dead," she said, and slipped by him to walk up the trail.

CHAPTER 10

KATE'S GRANDMOTHER SAT where she'd always sat, in a chair backed up against the wall between the oil stove and the kitchen table, knees wide apart, her right arm on the table, her left hand planted on her left knee.

Kate entered the room with slow, reluctant steps, pausing on the threshold. She stood where she was, head down. Her shoulders were slumped; her hands hung limply at her sides. Her gloves dangled from one, her face mask from the other. She didn't unzip her snowsuit. "I have come to tell you that Abel is dead."

Her grandmother rose ponderously to her feet and padded to the stove to put the water on to boil with slow, sure movements that argued the observance of a lifetime's rite.

"You knew, didn't you, emaa." It wasn't a question, it was a simple declaration of truth. "I think you might even be an accessory after the fact."

The old woman smiled into the teakettle. "Are you going to arrest me, Katya?" She reached above her head and took down two mugs and the Nestle's Quik. She went to the refrigerator and brought out a can of evaporated milk. She lifted the stove lid out of the way and set the teakettle directly over the flame.

"Why, emaa? Why didn't you just tell me?"

"I had no proof," the old woman said simply, without

turning from her task. "I knew how the old man felt about the boy's plans. I heard both of them testify before the subcommittee that afternoon. I saw the boy drive through the village toward Abel's house early the next morning. You know I don't sleep much anymore." She paused, looking down at the spoon she held. "And then the boy was missing. That was all."

"And when Ken Dahl came to you for help?"

Her grandmother turned and fixed her with the light brown eyes so like her own. "I told him nothing. It is not the business of Outsiders to meddle in our affairs."

Kate knuckled her eyes, which were dry and burning. She was unable to make them focus on any one thing. Her gaze skipped around the room, table to window, window to door, anything to keep her from looking at Ekaterina. She put her hands up to her face and spoke into them. "Couldn't you have warned him, emaa?"

"It is not the business of Outsiders to meddle in our affairs," her grandmother repeated in the same stern voice.

Kate gave a short laugh, high-pitched and too close to hysteria. "Even if one of our own is guilty of murder?"

"A park ranger, born and educated Outside," her grandmother said, her voice so indifferent it held not even the slightest trace of scorn. "A cheechako. And an investigator from Anchorage, much the same." Ekaterina shrugged. She might as well have snapped her fingers. "And now the man who killed them is dead."

"Abel," Kate said steadily. "Abel is dead, emaa. He had a name."

"They are all dead, Katya. What does it matter now?"

And what about me, emaa? Kate wanted to shout. What about me? I practically saw Abel die, and you as good as sent me there to do so! But she had no energy for anger this day.

The old woman was silent. "You should never have gone away to school, Katya," she said at last. She turned and fixed her granddaughter with a cool, considering stare that Kate had never seen before. "Or you should never have come back."

Kate's breath caught in her ruined throat. "The unkindest cut of all," she said finally, with a painful smile. "Why did you want me to think Martin killed Miller?"

"Because I knew that it was not true."

"And if I had not discovered that?"

"Then you would have removed Martin from the Park."

Kate expelled her breath on a long, soundless sigh. "Ridding Niniltna of a known troublemaker, and without you raising a finger in the process." She shook her head. "Did you think I wouldn't find out the truth?"

"I did not know if you would. I hoped not, for my cousin's husband's sake."

"What did you think would happen if I did?"

Her grandmother was silent for a moment. "I knew the old man would never go to jail." The teakettle whistled and she turned to remove it from the flame. "It is finished," she said, her back to her granddaughter. "Leave it. You can't change anything that has happened. We will drink some cocoa and eat some bread, and talk of other things."

Kate looked at the old woman, so strong, so proud, so righteous. Watching her, feeling off-balance and disoriented and one step removed from reality, she wondered idly if that was how she would feel drunk. "Jack is going to give Xenia a receptionist's job in Anchorage, emaa," she said. "He knows of another young woman in his office who needs someone to share rent. I've made conditions; for starters, she has to sign up for and pass with a C or better at least three credits every semester at UAA."

181

The old woman's back stiffened, and her voice was stern and disapproving. "You are taking her out of the only home she has ever known, away from family and friends."

"I'm getting her away from you," Kate said flatly.

Ekaterina turned and met her eyes. They were two women so alike, and at the same time so completely different. The chasm of more than a generation yawned between them and they stared at each other from opposite sides of the abyss. Kate, though the other woman had not spoken, shook her head. "No," she said, and then in a stronger voice repeated, "No. I'm not packing any more guilt out of here than I came in with. Good-bye, emaa."

Jack and Mutt were waiting outside the house. They drove back to Bobby's house and dropped off his Polaris. Kate took Jack up behind her and drove him to the airstrip, Mutt loping along next to them, her tongue hanging out, her head never very far from Kate's elbow.

Jack dismounted next to his Cessna, and stood with his eyes fixed on her set, white face. "Did she know?"

"Yes." Kate let the engine drop down to an idle.

Jack drew in a long, slow breath. "Makes her some kind of accessory."

"That's what I told her."

"What did she say?"

Kate laughed shortly. "She suggested I arrest her."

Jack scratched his head. "Uh-huh."

"Yeah, that's what I thought." They stood without speaking for a moment, and then Kate said, "Did you ever notice? To everyone else in the world, I'm Kate. Emaa calls me Katya."

"She's getting to you, Kate. Or trying to."

Kate kept talking, compulsively, the words spilling out of her as if he had not spoken. "Every time she says it, 'Katya,' she says it in that voice of doom. I see fifty generations of Aleuts lined up behind her, glaring at me. Every time she says it, she's telling me I betrayed her and my family and the village and my culture and my entire race by running away." She gave a thin smile. "And now, she's believes I've betrayed myself by running back. I've been preaching, and I quote, 'assimilation into the prevailing culture for the survival of my people.' Sounds pretty good, doesn't it? Sounds like I've had seven or eight sociology classes. Sounds like I know what I'm talking about." Kate smiled, and Jack winced away from the sight of it. "And I live in a log cabin five miles from my closest neighbor and twenty-five miles from the nearest village. I'm shipping Xenia off to town, but I can't bear to go in myself."

"Kate," he said.

"Don't you understand, we're not all like this," she said fiercely. "We're not even mostly like this. We're not all drunks and adulterers and murderers. We're just people, like anybody else trying to get along in this goddam world. We're starting from behind and we're just trying to catch up."

"Kate," he said again, reaching for her.

She held up her hands, holding him off. "Get out of the Park, Jack," she said in a tired voice. "You don't belong here."

"Do you?"

She shook her head again without answering, called to Mutt, and left.

• • •

It was a month before he came, out of the south, a big man in a parka with a wolf ruff, alone on a snow machine that threatened to destroy once and for all the peace of the little homestead in the clearing. Mutt shoved her way past her mistress and galloped out to him, her huge pads kicking up miniature clouds of the new snow that lay thick upon the ground.

"Hey, Mutt," he said, scratching the dog's head.

Kate stood motionless next to the open door, arms wrapped around herself. She was shivering and, realizing it, was angry with herself and with him. "What are you doing here?"

He walked to the cabin and gave her a gentle shove inside. He hung his parka next to hers, and sat down on the couch to unlace his mukluks. He set them carefully, one at a time, below his parka, not looking at her because it hurt him to see her so thin and tired. She looked as if she hadn't slept since he saw her last.

"I said, what are you doing here?" she repeated.

"Every couple of weeks, I think you said." He reached for her.

"No," she said and made a halfhearted attempt to push him away. Ignoring her, he pulled her into his arms, pushed her chin up with one firm hand and kissed her. In spite of his outward assurance she felt his body tense in awareness at the touch of hers. It might have been just a reflection of his own need, it might only have been pity, but with a sensation of coming home after a long, cold journey into foreign and unfriendly lands, she relaxed and leaned into the kiss. He pulled her head into his shoulder and for the first time she allowed herself the luxury of grief, great, racking sobs that tore at her wounded throat and at his heart.

"The funeral was last Wednesday," she said, when she could.

"I know. There was a big write-up about it in both Anchorage papers."

"I counted over a hundred planes parked on the airstrip

the day of the funeral. More than I've ever seen at his Fourth of July fly-ins."

"Well. It's one kind of testimonial."

"The one he would have liked best." Her voice was muffled in his shirt. "He left instructions that he wasn't to be buried in the family plot. He'd picked out a space on top of the hill in back of the house, underneath a big spruce. When Abel Junior and Zach started to dig the hole they found this enormous rock. They couldn't go through it or around it. They finally had to blow it out of the way with dynamite." Jack's chest shifted and she realized he was laughing, and she smiled in spite of herself. "Everyone said it was Abel's last laugh."

They sat quietly, listening to the fire crackle in the wood stove. Mutt curled up in front of it, her head on her paws, relaxed now that Kate was back in Jack's lap and all was right with the world.

"We sent Ken home to Boston," Jack said, "and Miller back to his daddy. The honorable representative from Ohio was inclined to make a fuss at first, but the press doesn't look kindly on congressmen drafting the FBI into investigating their personal affairs. All Gamble had to do was work the *Washington Post* into the conversation and Miller deflated like a stuck balloon."

"And Ken's people?"

Jack shook his head. "They don't make anything as vulgar as a fuss in Boston. I went out for the funeral. The sky wore gray; everyone else wore black. And pearls. Even the guys."

"Even the guys?"

"Cuff links. Tie tacks."

"Oh."

"Afterward, there was a reception at his parents' home,

185

where no one drank too much or cried out loud. When it was over, his mother thanked me for coming all that way. His father shook my hand. His brother drove me to the airport and carried my bag to the counter." Jack's voice hardened. "I'd have felt a whole lot better if someone had taken a punch at me."

They sat for a while, not moving. When she spoke again her ruined voice was so low he couldn't hear her. "What?" he said.

"Thanks," she said, louder but still gruff.

"For what?" he said, with more than a trace of bitterness in his voice. "Ekaterina was right. They're all dead. There was no point in the whole story making the ten o'clock news."

"Well. Thanks, anyway."

He looked down at her. "Will you come back to work for me?" he said.

"No," she said at once. "I'll never live in Anchorage again."

He looked at her for a long, searching moment. When he was done, he sighed, a long, drawn-out sigh, and nodded once, accepting her decision without comment.

"But I'll work for you sometimes. When you need someone who knows the Park. Who's related to half the bush." She raised her head and added, "For four hundred a day, plus expenses."

He had to grin. "Good enough." He slid one gentle, seeking hand over a breast. "It has nothing to do with this," he said. There would be no mistake. He wanted her. He had only been waiting.

"No," she agreed on a long sigh, arching her back and rubbing herself against his hands. She pulled his head down and kissed him. It had been too long, and she had missed this so much, and they'd always fit together so well. Nothing else mattered.

"Kate," he said, pulling back. "I came to Alaska because I wanted to see what it was like to live in a last frontier. I stayed because I wanted you. Just so you know, I feel pretty much the same today."

"All right," she said, unzipping his jeans and sliding one hand inside.

His hands closed around her upper arms in a painful grip. "I'll be out whenever I can get away."

"Yes."

He sighed beneath the touch of her hand. "Did you hear anything I just said?"

"No."

"Okay."

It wasn't going to get any better than this. He was a beggar at the gates, and he knew it. They had just opened, and if he hadn't been deeded the castle at least Kate had come down from her tower. He would take what he could get, and be grateful for it, and show his gratitude as well as he knew how.

He followed her up the ladder to the loft and into her large, lonely bed, and if it wasn't making love, it was as close to it as either one of them would ever get.

AFTERWORD

The phone rang on February 1, 1994. "Dana!" my editor cried. "You've been nominated for an Edgar!"

"Great!" I said. "What's an Edgar?"

There was a moment of silence, followed by a spluttering explanation. The Edgar Awards were to crime fiction what the Academy Awards were to film. Then a tentative, "You know what an Academy Award is, don't you?"

They were also, my editor said, flying me to New York City for the Edgar awards ceremony. When I finally figured out I had to dress up for it, I nearly said I couldn't go. For one thing, I was broke, and for another, I don't do dress-up. Not unless it's at gunpoint.

Which this pretty much was, so I went down to Nordstrom in Anchorage and found a pair of dress slacks with pockets (very important) on the sale rack. A top to match was much harder, and by the final week before Departure Day I was starting to panic.

I finally found a dress on some sale rack that fit my budget (seventy percent off) and looked marginally okay. I took it home and cut it off to just below waist length. I went to J.C. Penny's and found a couple of fake gold chains and hemmed them inside the bottom of what was now a top. (Sometimes I really shouldn't read. This time the culprit was a bio of Coco

Chanel, which informed me that she used metal chains to make her famous jackets hang just right. Well, what the hell, if it worked for Chanel...)

I think my black flats were from Payless ($10), and I found a pair of flashy rhinestone earrings and a couple of flashier rhinestone brooches in a junk shop. I was ready.

So the following week there I was, in the Edgar hotel in a corner room with a view all the way to Ohio. My best friend Kathy abandoned her husband and family to support me. The afternoon of the awards ceremony was sunny and warm and she said, "Statue of Liberty?"

"Statue of Liberty," I said, and we grabbed a cab to Battery Park and a ferry to Liberty Island. We wandered around in the footsteps of our ancestors until about four o'clock, when we boarded a very full, very slow ferry back to Manhattan over oily flat seas, the saucy tang of diesel very much in the air. People were sick over the side. I was not one of them, barely.

Back at Battery Park, we discovered much to our dismay that, A, four o'clock was also the time that nearby Wall Street shut down, so cabs were very thin on the ground, and B, it was shift change for what cabs there were and they weren't taking fares that didn't point them towards home anyway.

Neither of us spoke subway at the time, so we waved down cab after cab, only to have them say "Nahhh" when we told them where we were going. I started to think that if we ever did get a cab I should just head for the airport, because my publisher was footing what had to be a pretty spectacular bill and they were going to hurt me pretty badly when I didn't show up at the awards ceremony to graciously lose in person.

Finally, in an action that demonstrates precisely why she will forever be my best friend, Kathy leaped in front of a cab going the average New York City speed limit of 103MPH and forced it to a literally screeching halt. She marched around to the driver's side and said, "You WILL take us to our hotel."

He was so scared of her he did.

My first mandatory appearance was at a 5:30pm cocktail party. We came out of the elevator on our floor at fifteen minutes after five, undressing as we ran toward our room. We didn't even have time for showers, so I did a quick swipe with a wet washcloth and threw on my clothes and back to the elevator we went.

We walked into the reception. Everyone there was dressed like they had just wandered off the set of Dynasty. I'd never seen so many tuxes in one room in my life.

The one distinct memory I have of that evening lends to the general feeling of unreality I was experiencing. Donald Westlake was the grandmaster that year, and he called us his tribe. He said it twice, and thumped the podium, to make sure we got it. All the writers in the room were his, Donald Westlake's, tribe. Up until then little Dana Stabenow from Seldovia, Alaska had been a clan of one, and suddenly, I had family. Starting with the progenitor of Dortmunder.

And then they called my name. From. Up. There.

By that point I wasn't really in my body, but, sunburned, still a little sweaty, still a little seasick, clad in cut-off dress and rhinestones, I wobbled up on stage and grasped in a shaky hand an award the existence of which I had been completely unaware only three months before.

NEW YORK TIMES BESTSELLING AUTHOR

DANA STABENOW

'ONE OF THE STRONGEST VOICES IN CRIME FICTION' *SEATTLE TIMES*

A FATAL THAW

Eleven days ago Roger McAniff bought a new rifle.
Now nine people are dead, but only eight were killed
by McAniff...

CHAPTER 1

IT WAS SIX A.M. on the first day of spring, and although sunrise was still half an hour away, when Kate opened her eyes the loft of the cabin was filled with the cool, silvery promise of dawn. She sat up, stretched and yawned, and flung back the covers.

Pulling sweats on over her long underwear, she shimmied down the ladder from the loft into the cabin's single, square room. "Hey, girl." Mutt stood pressed up against the door, ears cocked, iron-gray ruff standing straight up around her face, yellow eyes wide and fixed imploringly on Kate. "In a minute. Hang on."

Going to the stove, Kate opened the fire door and stoked the fire from the wood bin next to it. The coals from the night before were still hot and it only took a moment for the wood to catch. She went to the sink and pumped up some water to replace what had evaporated out of the gallon-sized kettle overnight. Straining a little, she set it back on top of the stove. "Okay, girl," she said. Mutt danced with impatience as Kate stamped her bare feet into boots, and then, as Kate got down the choke chain and leash, her tail went between her legs and she whined, a soft, piteous sound.

"Forget it," Kate said severely. The scar on her throat, a whitish, flattened rope of twisted tissue stretching from ear to ear, pulled at her vocal chords in protest at this early-morning use, and her voice rasped like a rusty file over her next words. "I saw that old he-wolf hanging around yesterday. I know you're looking to get that itch of yours scratched but the last thing we need underfoot is a litter of pups." Mutt flattened her ears and furiously wagged an ingratiating tail. "Don't try that sweet talk on me. I remember what happened last time even if you don't."

Mutt heard the inflexible note in Kate's voice. Her tail stilled, her muzzle drooped and she gave a deep sigh. Conveying the impression that she had been beaten into it, she submitted meekly to the leash, and slunk through the door and around the woodpile.

Kate let the leash run all the way out to give her some privacy and waited. She breathed in deeply of the cool morning air, smelling of pine resin and wood smoke. The big, round, flat-faced thermometer fixed to the wall of the cabin read twelve degrees, and it was only six-thirty. Yes, spring was finally here, at last.

She felt a single, experimental tug on the leash. One large yellow eye peered over the woodpile. "Not a chance," Kate told her, and took her turn in the outhouse without loosing her grip on the leash.

• • •

The killer woke a few moments later, twenty-five miles to the east, and rose at once, whistling. He washed his face and brushed his teeth, slowly methodically, a deliberate ceremony to his movements. Shaving was almost a ritual, and he was very careful not to nick himself with the blade. The new clothes—Levis, a Pendleton shirt, socks, T-shirt, shorts, bought

2

the day before in Niniltna—had been painstakingly laid out on his bed in the order that he would put them on.

The clerk at Niniltna General Store hadn't recognized him yesterday, in spite of his shopping there all winter long. He wiped the last of the shaving cream from his face and smiled at himself in the mirror.

● ● ●

Kate ate the last of last week's bread as toast dunked in her morning coffee. She mixed up a batch of dough and turned it into a buttered bowl. Covering it with a damp kitchen towel she sat it next to the wood stove to rise. Puttering around the cabin, she changed the sheets on the bed in the loft and the towels next to the sink, scoured out the sink, cleaned the top of the stove, took the rag rugs outside to shake, and swept the hardwood floor. Pumping up enough water to fill the washtub, she added soap and clothes and left it on the wood stove to heat through. She cleaned the chimneys and trimmed the wicks of all the propane lamps. It was her usual Monday morning routine and she performed it on automatic. It was good to have a routine. It got things done, and it kept her too busy to think too much on how isolated she was. In the middle of 20 million square acres of national park in Alaska, where her closest neighbors were the grizzly sow across the river just waking up after a long winter's nap and the he-wolf sniffing hopefully around her horny husky, if she let herself she could get to feeling pretty lonely. Kate never gave herself enough time to feel lonely.

Chores complete, she sat down at the table next to the oil cookstove and pulled the one-pound Darigold butter can toward her. Dumping it out, she began to separate bills and stack coins. When she was through she had the grand sum of $296.61.

"Well," she told Mutt, "better than at breakup last year. At least we're going into this spring solvent."

Mutt wagged her tail in halfhearted agreement.

● ● ●

The Winchester Model 70 30.06 was new, purchased just the day before, from the same general store in Niniltna that had sold him his new clothes, from the same incurious clerk. The bullets were new as well, a dozen cardboard boxes of shiny new cartridges, 180-grain hunting ammunition, Winchester (he was loyal to the brand) Super X Silvertips, twenty rounds to the box. He succumbed to temptation and opened one of the boxes, pulling out a round. Even in that early light the brass gleamed, the copper glowed and the silver shone. He'd never seen anything so beautiful.

He set up a row of empty cans and bottles on a sawhorse placed across the road leading to the lane outside his cabin. From the crossbar he hung a paper target, a series of concentric circles.

He paced off 150 yards down the old, straight railroad bed that served as the Park's main, and only, road. The hard-packed snow of winter was beginning to melt and break up beneath his feet. He squatted and set the boxes of ammunition to one side. Taking the rifle in both hands, he held it to his face for a moment, inhaling the fragrance of the oiled walnut stock, running an adoring fingertip down the gleaming black barrel. The bolt worked smoothly, the craftsmanship of the piece evident in each planed and polished surface, all the machined parts working together to form a perfect whole.

He pulled the stock firmly into his shoulder and sighted down the barrel. The tiny metal bead at the end of the barrel seemed at once so close and so far away. The metal was so new it glistened in the early morning light. He frowned, and felt around in his pockets for a match. Striking it, he held it so the smoke rising from it blackened the bead.

He looked at the factory sights and shook his head with an indulgent smile. From another pocket he produced a Williams Foolproof peephole sight and mounted it next to the receiver. He loaded the rifle, five in the magazine, one in the chamber, and stood. He pulled the stock in tight and sighted through the aperture, noting that in spite of the overwhelming whiteness of the surrounding snow pack the dulled black bead at the end of the barrel stood out clearly, with no distracting reflection of light. He squeezed off six shots, enjoying the cracking sound of the reports, the solid thump of the butt into his shoulder, the smooth action of the bolt between rounds. When the chamber was empty, he walked back up the road and inspected the target. Most of his shots were grouped above and to the left of the bull's-eye. He adjusted the peephole sight with a small screwdriver, reloaded, and repeated the process. The third time he shot at the bottles and cans.

It took him less than an hour. When he was done, he had a killing machine that would reduce the three hundred yards between target and shooter to point-blank range. "A dead shot," he said, and smiled. And his wife had accused him of having no sense of humor.

He reloaded, and was careful to switch on the safety afterward. He didn't want to hurt himself.

● ● ●

"No, I said, and no, I meant," Kate told the door. Mutt whined mournfully behind it. "Besides, take it from me, men are nothing but trouble."

She pulled hard on the knob to see that the door had, in fact, truly latched, and turned to walk to the garage. Its double doors swung open easily, now that a winter's worth of ice and snow packed around the sill had melted down.

The building was an unheated shell made of three-by-six sheets of plywood on a frame of two-by-fours. A row of windows, encrusted with a year's worth of grime and mosquitoes, shed little light on the interior. The inside was lined with long strips of fuzzy pink fiberglass insulation between the studs, and shelves bolted to the studs, floor to ceiling and wall to wall. The floor was made of rough, unplaned planks. There was a red metal tool chest as tall as Kate mounted on wheels standing in one corner, a table saw in another and a counter with a line of power tools hanging from a pegboard nailed up above it. Unfinished and utilitarian, the garage was neat, reasonably clean and arranged so that everything in it was immediately ready to hand. Kate swept the tools with a stern eye and was satisfied that none of them had rehung themselves carelessly in her absence.

She went around the snow machine parked in front to the pickup truck behind it. It was a small diesel, an Isuzu Trooper, with a homemade toolbox mounted in the bed behind the cab. She popped the hood. She'd disconnected but not removed the battery when the first big snow fell the previous autumn. Now she took it out and set it on the counter. She left the garage and went to the generator shed. The Onan 3.5KW had been new last fall, but it was also diesel and balked at an easy start as a matter of principal. She bled off some air from the compression-release valve and, grunting, gave the hand crank a few more turns. The engine caught, and she winced away from the resulting roar. She shut the door on it and returned to the garage. A single, 150-watt light bulb she had forgotten to turn off in February lit up the dim interior. She hooked the truck battery up to the trickle charger and left it.

As an afterthought she went around to the back of the cabin and climbed the wooden ladder to the rack that held the diesel fuel tanks, a dozen fifty-five gallon Chevron drums mounted on their sides, connected with lengths of insulated copper tubing to each other, the cabin and the generator shack. Pulling the dipstick from its rack next to the ladder, she tested each barrel. The diesel was used only to run the truck, the cabin's oil stove and the generator to run the power tools in the garage, so the barrels were all about a quarter to a third full. It was enough to see her through to late May or early June, when the road opened up and the tanker from Ahtna could get through. "Close enough for government work," she said out loud, and wiped the dipstick and capped the last barrel.

She went back into the house and reappeared with a bucket of soapy water, a sponge and a squeegee and began to wash the windows on the garage. After a while the sun grew warm enough to remove her sweatshirt and work in shirtsleeves. "Bet we hit thirty-five today," she said. She stopped and looked guiltily at the cabin. Huge yellow eyes stared reproachfully out at her from the window over the sink. "Get your paws off the counter, dammit," Kate called, but her heart wasn't in it. Something halfway between a whine and a howl was the reply, and she sighed and put down the squeegee.

Mutt greeted her at the door with ecstatic yips and tried to weasel her way outside. Kate wound one hand in her ruff and with the other reached for the choke chain and leash. She led Mutt outside, slipped the choke chain around Mutt's cringing neck and fastened the leash to a length of wire stretched between two trees at the edge of the clearing. The leash was just long enough to let Mutt run up and down the length of the wire without tangling itself. Mutt immediately dropped to her belly and, without a trace of shame, groveled for freedom.

"Don't look like that," Kate told her. "You know it's for your own good."

• • •

The killer donned hat and jacket and gloves and shouldered the rifle. He took the little mirror from its nail on the wall and held it at arm's length to survey his appearance. He frowned and made a minute adjustment to the collar of his shirt. His brows puckered a little over the wrinkling effect of the rifle's strap on his new mackinaw. He smoothed the jacket down with one hand, readjusted the strap just a hair to the left, and was satisfied.

He looked around the cabin. It was spotless, the chipped white porcelain of the sink scrubbed clean, the stove top scoured and gleaming blackly, the floor swept, the bunk made up neatly beneath its olive-drab army blanket. He nodded his head, pleased. No one was ever going to be able to say he wasn't a good housekeeper.

His first stop was a mile down the road. He enjoyed the walk, the cool, calm air, the chittering of the squirrels. Once he paused and cocked his head, certain that he'd heard a golden-crowned sparrow trill out its trademark three descending notes, Spring Is Here. It didn't repeat itself, and he moved on.

When he came into the clearing of the next cabin down the road, he met his neighbor coming in from the outhouse. He was greeted, if not with enthusiasm, then at least with civility. "Hey, hi there. Great first day of spring, isn't it? Want some coffee?"

He turned toward the cabin and the first bullet caught him in the back, severing his spinal cord and exploding out of his chest in a hole six inches across. The second bullet went in the back of his neck and ripped out the front of his throat, changing his last terrified scream into a bubbling gurgle of bewilderment.

• • •

The sun was high and warm in a clear, pastel sky, and the thermometer on the cabin wall read twenty-eight above. "Told you so," she said to Mutt. Setting the chisel with a few taps of the blunt side of the axe, she stood back, raised the axe over her head, and brought the blunt side down on the chisel. The round of pine had seasoned through the winter and split cleanly at the first blow, with a satisfying crack, into two almost even halves. "I'm giving a loose to my soul," she told Mutt. Mutt yawned and settled her chin on crossed forepaws. Her choke chain was pulled tight, her leash stretched as far as it would go between choke chain and wire, and the leash run as far as it could get from where Kate was chopping wood. She was not speaking to Kate, but she still had plenty to say, all of it eloquent. Properly chastened, Kate reversed the axe and used the blade to split each half into two chunks.

A jangle of chain and a flurry of hysterical barks interrupted the splitting of the second round. She looked up to see Mutt prancing frantically, in a manner wholly unsuited to her age and dignity, at the extreme end of the wire closest to the edge of the clearing. Every hair on her body strained against the leash. Kate followed her gaze and drew in a breath.

He was a timber wolf, ash gray in color, standing three and a half feet tall at the shoulder and weighing, Kate estimated, a hundred and sixty pounds. His eyes were large, brown and probably usually filled with intelligence. Today they were bright with something else, and they were fastened on the half-wolf, half-husky tethered to the wire next to Kate's cabin. He shook his coat into amorous order, adjusted the curl of his tail and stalked forward.

He was, all in all, a very handsome fellow indeed. Well, Mutt was no hag herself, and Kate understood the impetus behind and almost wavered beneath the onslaught of imploring yips and entreating howls from both lovers. She managed to pull herself together, though, and spoke in a stern voice. "Dammit, Mutt, I told you. We don't need any more puppies around here. The last bunch like to drove both of us into running away from home. We're lucky they turned out to be halfway trainable so Mandy could put them to work."

Mutt ignored the voice of reason, quivering, her ruff standing straight up, her tail curled coquettishly, her wide yellow eyes fixed on the wolf. He paused in his approach, glancing for the first time in Kate's direction, taking her in at a single glance and dismissing her as negligible. Kate wasn't quite sure she even registered on his peripheral vision as human and therefore a potential threat; his attention was clearly fixed elsewhere.

She moved over to the wire. Mutt danced around her eagerly, and Kate took one cautionary wind of the leash around her forearm, regarded it for a moment and took another. "Never underestimate the power of love," she muttered, and Mutt proved her point by almost jerking her arm out of its socket when Kate detached the leash from the

10

wire. Mutt pulled avidly for the trees, Kate grimly for the cabin. Sweating, straining, and swearing all the way, the tug-of-war turned her hands and forearm dark red and numb to all feeling. Finally, Kate managed to get her shivering, whining roommate back inside and the cabin door safely closed and latched behind her. She subsided limply on the doorstep and mopped her overheated brow. "Besides," she told the eager scrabble of toenails against the other side of the door, "if I can do without, so can you."

From the edge of the clearing the wolf howled, a long, lovelorn sound that rose to a frustrated crescendo. "Oh, shut up," Kate snapped, and returned to vent her spleen on the woodpile.

• • •

"Well, hey there, my first customer of the morning." The portly, cheerful man turned to face him across the counter. "The mail plane hasn't been in yet, so—"

The killer shot once. The expanding nose of the soft-tipped bullet shredded the back of the man's head and stuccoed the wall of wooden cubbyholes behind him in grayish white and dark red. The man's body stood, swaying for a moment, before slumping slowly and somehow gracefully to the floor.

There was a still, silent moment. The killer heard a quick, sharp intake of breath and wheeled to see the curtain that separated the post office from the rest of the house moving, as if someone had been holding it open and had just released it. He jerked it back, to reveal an empty living room, the door to it swinging wide. He went to the door and looked out, and saw her running down the long, narrow length of the airstrip, a pudgy little gray-haired woman in jeans and sweatshirt and

11

stocking feet. He thought she screamed. A movement caught his eye and he looked beyond her. Two people on a snow machine broke out of the trees at the middle of the strip. The running woman yelled and waved her arms. The driver looked her way and turned the snow machine in her direction. The woman screamed and waved her arms more frantically.

The killer brought the 30.06 to his shoulder in one smooth motion and shot once. The driver slumped over the handlebars and the machine swerved abruptly. The passenger screamed and tried to shove the driver aside so she could grasp the handlebars, to no avail. She screamed again, and went on screaming, as the machine slewed and swerved, back and forth, across the airstrip. Lining up the sight, the killer exhaled, held it and shot again. The screaming stopped abruptly. The snow machine, riderless, ran into the plowed snowbank at the side of the strip and flipped over.

He gave the Winchester a fond pat and looked around for the running woman. He found her all the way down at the end of the strip, stubby legs pumping tirelessly beneath the spur of adrenaline. Sighting carefully through the peephole, down the barrel and over the darkened bead that stood out so clearly against the hard-packed snow of the runway, he closed his fingers almost gently around the trigger, heard the shot and its echo immediately following, felt the kick of the butt against his shoulder, saw her stagger and fall. She lay still for a moment, before lifting herself up on her forearms and dragging herself into the trees. He shook his head, almost in admiration, and went after her.

He paused at the edge of the strip to look at the bodies of the two from the snow machine. He turned them face up with one foot, careful not to let the blood dull the gloss of his new boots. One body no longer had a face, the other no chest. The

12

killer straightened one's shirt, the other's legs, and followed the tracks into the trees.

A sharp crack echoed through the woods, and instinctively he threw himself down and rolled. He came up shooting, working the bolt and spacing his shots in an arc. He paused to reload, listening. There was complete silence, and then he saw the broken branch in one of his own footprints. He clucked at his over-reaction and recovered her trail. A few yards down it, he found the body.

He approached cautiously, rifle held in front of him, a round in the chamber and the safety off. Mukluks, bright pink bib overalls, a checked shirt. "Oh," he said, on a long note of discovery when at last he saw her face, and sank to his knees, beside her in the stained snow.

She was blonde and she was beautiful, even in death. The last time he'd seen her, that fair skin had been flushed, the full, red lips twisted away from her white, straight teeth in a sneer, the widely-spaced dark blue eyes narrowed in contempt. She had laughed at him.

He smiled down at her now, touched her cheek. It was cooling rapidly. He raised one lid to see if her eye was as blue as he remembered. It was. He admired the perfect fans her thick lashes made on her cheeks. His hand slid down her throat, shaped one breast, stroked her narrow waist, cupped between her thighs.

A small whisper, perhaps of wind, rustled through the grove. A sound, perhaps the whimper of a frightened squirrel, came from deeper in the stand of trees. It was enough to make him withdraw his hand.

He rose to his feet and threaded his way through the trees to the airstrip. Righting the overturned snow machine, he mounted it and thumbed the electric starter. It caught on the first try.

●●●

The pile of split wood was waist high when Kate heard the rapid whap-whap-whap of a helicopter's rotor. The sun was high in a still-cloudless sky, and her shirt was damp down her spine and beneath her arms. She sunk the axe into the tree stump that served as her chopping block and went inside to pump up a drink of water. She drained the glass, refilled it and brought it back outside, narrowly missing Mutt's nose in the door. She sat down on the front step, groaning a little from sore muscles. A rustle of underbrush called her attention to the edge of the clearing, where Mutt's would-be lover sat beneath a mountain hemlock. For a change he was not looking yearningly at the cabin but in an inquiring fashion at the sky. She squinted up as the noise of the helicopter became louder, and jumped to her feet when it roared the last few feet to hover over her clearing.

"What the hell do you think you're doing?" she yelled, her voice a furious croak. "You can't land here!"

Mutt's lover decided it was a better day for discretion than valor and broke for the high country. As the Bell Jet Ranger with the distinctive blue-and-gold markings of the Alaska State Troopers lowered to the exact center of the clearing, Kate was forced back up against the door of the cabin. She held her breath, watching the ends of the rotors sweep dangerously close to the eaves of every building in the semicircle of her homestead.

The blades slowed their rotation but didn't stop. The engine powered down, and the door of the helicopter opened and a man in a state trooper's uniform emerged. Holding on to his hat, he crouched over the few running steps that brought him face to crotch with Kate.

14

She glared down at him. "What the hell do you think you're doing, Jim? You're lucky you didn't take the roof off everything I own!"

"Get inside!" he yelled, and suited word to deed by reaching around her to open the door and shove her inside, thudding up the steps and in behind her and pulling the door shut after him.

He was a tall man and a large one, and he filled up the cabin more than she liked. "What the hell do you think you're doing," she snapped, "pushing your way in here? What's going on?"

"You haven't heard?"

"Heard what?"

He strode over to her scanner and snapped it on, to be greeted by dead air. He shook his head and swore. "Dammit, I told them to broadcast a warning and keep broadcasting it until we catch the fucker."

"What fucker? What warning?" she said angrily. And then she saw his expression. In that instant her anger changed to apprehension. The words devoid of heat, she repeated. "Jim, what's going on?"

He turned and surveyed the room, Kate mystified, Mutt alert, both of them wary. "At least you're all right."

"Of course I'm all right." Kate's gaze sharpened. "Who isn't?"

His lips thinned. "Two people we know of, so far."

"Niniltna?" He nodded curtly, and she tensed. Next to her Mutt whined once, a keen, anxious sound. "What happened?" Kate said flatly.

He blew out a breath. "Near as we can figure, some guy's running around shooting at people with a 30.06."

Her mouth went dry. "Who?"

15

He shook his head. "We don't know yet."

"Who's been shot?"

A gleam of understanding crossed his face, but he shook his head again. "We don't that yet, either. He shot at the mail plane as it was coming in to land. George Perry saw some bodies lying at the end of the strip. Then a guy on a snow machine started shooting and he hit the throttle. He climbed to five thousand feet and circled long enough to put out an SOS. He saw the guy on the snow machine take off. That's about all we know, except..."

"Except?"

"Except that he's headed this way." The trooper saw Kate's reaction and nodded once for emphasis. "The mail plane called the tower in Tok, the tower called me, and I got in the air right away. I've been hitting every homestead on the way in."

Kate walked around him and got the shotgun down from the rack over the door. She broke it open to check that it was loaded. It was. She turned. "Okay. Now I know. You'd better get on with passing the word."

His expression relaxed, and he gave half a laugh and amazed her by swooping down for a swift, hard kiss. He laughed again at her expression and chucked her beneath the chin. "Probably the only chance I'll ever get, how could I resist?"

The shotgun was on its way up and if the helicopter hadn't been right in back of him she might even have fired off a round. He looked from her furious face to the shotgun and back, laughed again and actually had the gall to salute her. "If he gets here before I get him, he's wearing a black-and-red mackinaw and a brown billed cap with ear-flaps. He's driving a Polaris. Watch your ass, Shugak."

16

He ducked and ran to the helicopter. The engine pitch and blade rotation increased immediately. In five seconds he was in the air, in seven over the trees, and in ten out of sight.

• • •

"Go!" the farmer yelled at the two open-mouthed, petrified figures of his children. "Run, dammit!" He turned back to the killer and waved his arms. "Here! Over here, you lousy bastard! Come get me, I dare you!"

The killer looked at him without expression. The farmer, lying against his barn with a shattered leg and his life's blood oozing away, clutched frantically around him for something to throw. He found nothing but melting snow, and so he threw that, in handfuls that fell far short of their target in ineffective, disintegrating pieces. "Shit!" The killer watched him without moving. "Motherfucker!" the farmer yelled and flipped him the bird with both hands. "Joe! Mary! Run!"

The two children finally broke and ran, straight out across the frozen pond that fronted the farm buildings. The killer took half a step forward, swiveled and brought up the rifle. He frowned at the running figures through the sights. They were so small and they ran so fast. He squeezed off two shots. One hit, one missed. "No!" the farmer screamed, "no, no, no goddam you, no!" The killer shot a third time. The second figure fell hard on the grainy ice of the little lake and slid ten feet before coming to a stop.

The farmer, sobbing, crying, gasping for breath, was clawing his body to the edge of the lake when the killer stepped up next to him. Their eyes met. The killer's face was calm and still, the farmer's contorted with grief and rage.

"Fuck you," the farmer hissed. "Do it."

Kate leaned the shotgun against the woodpile and picked up the axe. After staring at it for a moment, she put the axe back down and picked up the shotgun. She felt like pacing, but pacing back and forth across the clearing with a crazy person going around shooting at people seemed like a bad idea. It might have been the safest thing to do, but she couldn't bear the thought of cooping herself up in the cabin. She turned to the woods. A frustrated whine and an eager scratching at the inside of the door told her Mutt had seen her. She paused. There was a rustle across the clearing. The timber wolf was back. "Damn." In the state she was in and with this embodiment of lupine perfection hanging around, Mutt would be no use to her. Squaring her shoulders, she walked across the clearing and up the path that led to the road.

• • •

The miner vanished into the trees as the killer reloaded the Winchester. The frantic, laboring sound of someone crashing through thick woods and a winter's worth of snow cover came clearly to him through the still air. He threw in the bolt and cast a speculative glance toward the sound. He stretched and yawned. The snow under the trees was too darn deep to hassle with. The miner would probably bleed to death anyway. Besides, he was tired. His stomach growled. Hungry, too.

• • •

Kate was dozing when she heard it. At first it had sounded like a single, distinct crash, like a large-scale breaking of glass, but now there was no doubt about it. It was a snow machine, and it was coming her way.

She'd walked from where the path that led to her homestead intersected the old railroad bed until she found a long, straight stretch of the road. At the end of the straight stretch farthest from Niniltna, she searched out a squat, thickly branched spruce tree that was neither too close nor too far away from the edge of the road, stamped out a path and forced her way in between the branches. She squatted beneath it now with the shotgun resting across her knees. Peering out between the branches, she had a perfect view of half a mile of road, from where it curved to avoid Honker Pond to where she crouched.

The noise of the snow machine grew louder. The sky was clear and pale and innocent of helicopters or planes or any other kind of cavalry. "Damn you, Jim. Isn't that just like a cop, never around when you need him." When she looked back down the snow machine had rounded Honker Pond and was headed straight for her. There was no one else in sight.

She muttered a curse and clicked the safety off the shotgun. She rechecked the load, pulled the stock in against her shoulder, sighted carefully down the barrel, and waited.

The snow machine labored up the slight slope, until she could see his face, red from the force of the wind against it, lips pulled back from his teeth in a humorless grimace. It was a Polaris snow machine, all right, and the guy was wearing a red-and-black checked mackinaw and a brown-billed cap with earflaps. A chill shivered down her spine. She took her time lining up her shot. No matter what this yo-yo had done, she didn't want to kill him. She had enough on her conscience without another death, however justified.

He was almost upon her when the snow of the road exploded in front of his machine. Pieces of ice flew up and hit the windshield and his face. He yelled and jerked. The machine swerved. The handlebars ripped out of his hands and he fell, rolling awkwardly, slung rifle and all.

Kate plunged out between the branches of the spruce. One caught in her hair and almost yanked her off her feet. She slipped and lost her grip on the shotgun. It smacked into the snow and slid several feet from her. Across the road, the killer staggered to his feet and unslung his rifle. She felt around and grasped a piece of deadwood and threw it at him as hard as she could. It caught him square across the face. He staggered a little. "Doggone it," he said. He recovered, and in one automatic action raised his rifle and sighted down at her.

Her hair still tangled in the spruce, the stock of the shotgun several feet away, Kate froze. She stared across the hard, packed roadbed into his calm, clear, quite mad eyes, and she knew she was staring at an escape from pain, a loss of laughter, the cessation of joy, all of them, straight in the face. She didn't move, couldn't.

He smiled at her. "Know anywhere around here somebody might get a bite to eat?"

There was a crash of tearing brush, and Kate was hit hard in the back of the knees. Her feet went out from under her, her hair ripped free of the branch and the world whirled around as she made a perfect backward somersault, landing on her chest with a thump that drove all the breath out of her.

Mutt's forepaws hit the killer square in the chest. He fell flat on his back with a hundred and forty pounds of proprietary rage on top of him. In a movement faster than Kate could follow Mutt clamped her teeth in the stock of the Winchester and shook it loose from his grip like a bear shaking off a mosquito. The rifle hit the ice six feet away and slid for twenty more. The killer lay where he was, dazed, his throat exposed, and Mutt lunged directly for it, her teeth closing in on either side.

Kate's breath returned with a rush. "Hold!" she shouted.

Mutt froze, her teeth indenting but not breaking the skin of his throat. "Hold, girl," Kate repeated, grasping at air, her voice a husky croak, "hold."

It took her two tries to climb to her feet. She stood where she was, trembling, eyes closed, gulping in great breaths of air. Her chest hurt. Her scalp ached. Her lungs burned. Somewhere behind them the Polaris was still running. The engine rose in whiny protest, spluttered and died. Kate sucked in another deep breath and opened her eyes.

The killer lay where he had fallen. Mutt stood over him, teeth bared against his throat, a low, rumbling growl issuing unbroken from deep in her throat. In that moment she seemed all wolf. Kate recovered her shotgun and approached them warily. She reached his rifle, kicked it away. "All right, Mutt."

The dog lifted her head slightly, her teeth no longer touching the killer's throat, but that continuous, rumbling, paralyzing growl never stopped. "It's all right, girl," Kate said and reached out a steadying hand. Beneath it Mutt flinched once, and Kate tensed. "You done good, girl. Now let go. Mutt," she repeated, more sternly this time, "release." The growl missed a note, diminished, and died. Mutt looked up at Kate and gave her tail a single wag. Kate inhaled again and straightened. "Good girl." And then, more fervently, "*Good* girl."

The killer was conscious. He looked up at them calmly, all tension drained out of his body. He even smiled, a happy, bloody smile that reached all the way up into mischievous, twinkling eyes, one nearly swollen shut. He giggled. "You'll never guess what I've been doing." He giggled again. "I've been a bad boy." He licked the blood from his lips and

21

appeared surprised. He raised one wondering hand, touched it to his mouth and looked at his stained fingers. "I'm bleeding," he said. His face puckered. "He should have sold me Boardwalk. I told him. He should have sold it to me." He started to cry.

Kate took three faltering steps to the side of the road and was thoroughly and comprehensively sick, which was how Chopper Jim found her when he landed twenty yards down the road a few minutes later.

CHAPTER 2

JACK MORGAN SIGHED. "It's too bad everyone lived right on the road. McAniff didn't have to go out of his way any to find targets."

"No."

Jack tilted his chair back and crossed his booted feet on the top of his desk. A pile of paper six inches high tilted and almost slipped to the floor. He didn't seem to notice, and Bill Robinson, grumbling beneath his breath, bent forward to straighten it. It still amazed him how Jack, chief investigator for the Anchorage District Attorney's office, could find anything in that office in time for trial. Small, square and windowless to begin with, it was made even smaller by the overflow of file cabinets, crime scene drawings, evidence bags, three chalkboards covered on both sides with his boss's scrawling script and a stack of paper that started somewhere near the door and rolled across the room in drifts, like snow after a blizzard, to engulf Jack's desk. More paper in the form of maps were tacked to every square inch of the walls, with crime scene drawings taped over every square inch of the maps, all heavily marked with more notes in Jack's illegible scrawl. Jack leaned toward the black, broad strokes of a Marksalot for arrows, exclamation points and marginal balloons.

Even Bill had to admit that Jack's conviction rate proved that he could and did find what he needed when he needed it, though only Jack and maybe God alone knew how. And it wasn't his office. He shook his head, not for the first time, and sat back in his chair to line up the corners on the neat stack of paper in his lap.

"Okay, Bill," Jack said, staring at the ceiling with his hands linked behind his head. "Run it down for me."

Bill turned a page, shuffled it to the bottom of the pile with meticulous precision, and cleared his throat. "His neighbor was the first to be hit. Name of Stephen Syms, 34. Lived in the Park year-round, fished in the summer, did what he could in the winter. His neighbors on the other side were the Getty sisters, Lottie and Lisa. They heard the shots at about ten A.M. and according to Lottie went over to take a look. By the time they got there, Stephen Syms was dead and McAniff gone. They looked for tracks and didn't find any, and there's only the one road, so they got out their snow machine and followed it into Niniltna."

Bill flipped a page. "Okay, scene shifts to Niniltna, post office next to the airstrip. Postmaster's name was Patrick Jorgensen, 63, moved to Niniltna in 1949, married, raised a family, been the postmaster there for the last twenty years. He was shot once at point-blank range. His wife, Becky Jorgensen, 64, saw it all from the next room and ran out the living room door and down the strip. McAniff must have heard something because he followed her out and shot at her, she thinks a couple of times." He looked up at Jack. "Her memory gets a little confused at this point, and who can blame her. He shot at her at least once, though, because she's got as neat a hole through her upper right arm as you ever saw. Swish, right through, didn't touch the bone or the artery." He shook his head.

24

"She was lucky."

"She wasn't the only one." He flipped to a third page. "About the time she got to the end of the strip—by the way, she couldn't tell me why she didn't duck into the trees on one side or the other. She just ran, flat out, trying to put as much distance between the rifle and her."

"Maybe between the mess it left of her husband of thirty-two years and her," Jack said gently.

"Maybe. It was a mess. So, she gets to the end of the strip and who should appear out of the trees but Lyle and Lucy Longstaff, both 24. He was a Park rat, hunted, fished, panned a little gold. She was a bank teller he met and married in Anchorage, on New Year's Day."

"This New Year?"

"Yeah."

"Jesus."

"Yeah. She quit her job in January and moved to his cabin down on Gold Creek. They'd come up to Niniltna to meet the mail plane." Bill was a square, stolid man with a square, stolid face without much expression. And yet, as Jack listened to him tick off the victims and their descriptions from his neatly typed list, Bill's counting-down acquired something of a dirge-like quality. In his careful enunciation of the names of the dead, in his use of their full names each time he said them, it was as if he were testifying to their very existence, to the space they had once occupied on the earth, in the only way he would permit himself. All cops know that emotional involvement in any case is fatal, to themselves and usually to the case. Many of them succeed in their work only by devising a kind of working separation of person and profession, sort of like church and state. Or they try to. The best succeed at least part of the time. And yet. And yet.

"So, McAniff shoots Lyle Longstaff and Lucy Longstaff; theirs are the two bodies George Perry, the mail plane pilot, saw lying at the end of the runway. McAniff went into the woods at the end of the runway after Becky Jorgensen, evidently shooting as he went, because here's where the fell hand of fate steps in.

"The Getty sisters made it in from Syms's cabin, and the first place they stop is the first place everybody stops coming into Niniltna."

"The post office."

"Right. They see Patrick Jorgensen laid out back of the counter and hear shooting down the runway. They split up and circle around the woods in back of the strip where they heard the shooting. McAniff lost Becky Jorgensen, then, and it looks like he lay down a screen of shots, trying to get her. Lottie Getty stumbled across Becky Jorgensen and they hightailed it out of there. It was just dumb bad luck Lisa Getty ran into one of McAniff's bullets." He paused. "She was a looker."

"I saw the pictures."

"Yeah. Thirty years old, looked like Marilyn Monroe, beauty spot, body and all. What a waste." Bill shook his head, and he turned to the next page. "So, Perry lines up for a final and all of a sudden finds the air over the strip filled with more bullets than a hot LZ and he was outa there."

"Understandable."

"He climbed out of range and circled for a while, looking down at the scene through binoculars. He saw McAniff head down the road to Ahtna, and he was the one who finally got a message through to Jim Chopin in Tok, who saddled up and headed out. Meanwhile, back at the massacre." He shuffled some more paper.

26

"John Weiss, thirty-seven, his wife Tina, thirty-five, and their two children, Mary, six, and Joseph, five, lived on a farm about ten miles out of Niniltna."

"Why didn't he shoot up the town when he went through?" Jack interjected.

"He didn't go through town, he went over the river and through the woods and picked up the road at Squaw Candy Creek."

Jack's feet came down with a thump. "Squaw Candy Creek. Bobby Clark lives on Squaw Candy Creek. Has anyone—"

"Black guy in a wheelchair, does the NOAA reporting from the Park?" Jack nodded, and Bill waved a reassuring hand. "He's okay. Chopper Jim checked on him." Bill gave a dour smile. "Jim says Clark was mad as hell that McAniff didn't come his way, he would have shown the fucker how fancy he could shoot."

Jack sighed with relief. "That's our Bobby. Thank God."

"The Weisses lived in another house by the side of the road. Apparently Tina Weiss caught it first, in the outhouse. Near as we can figure, McAniff shot John Weiss once in the left thigh, after which Mary and Joseph ran out onto a little lake the farmhouse fronted on. McAniff shot them as they were about to make the trees on the other side. It was almost like he waited until they got that far before shooting."

"Gave them a sporting chance," Jack suggested acidly. "Who does this guy think he is, General Zaroff?"

"From the evidence it looks more like he was seeing just how good a shot he was." He met Jack's eyes. "Small targets, moving, that kind of thing."

Jack closed his eyes and said wearily, "Jesus Christ."

"John Weiss, who we think was conscious and saw all this, was trying to crawl out to them when McAniff walked over

27

and shot him. One shot, right here." Bill demonstrated with a cocked finger to his left temple. "Point-blank range. Powder burns beneath the skin, casing next to the body. He just walked up, stared him straight in the eye, and shot him."

There was a brief pause as both men imagined the scene in their minds; the mother shot where she sat; the father allowed to live long enough to witness the cold and deliberate murder of his own children; the last, lone and by then probably welcome shot to the head. Jack's skin crawled, and he shook himself and got up to refill their cups. The coffee was hot and strong and burned going down, and it brought Jack back from that cold scene by the lake to the more prosaic surroundings of his crowded office.

"Next stop, the access road to the Nabesna Mine. It was just more dumb bad luck that had MacKay Devlin turning onto the road to Niniltna when McAniff passed by. He says he hung a right a little fast and skidded to a stop on the old railroad bed right in front of McAniff s snow machine. McAniff had the 30.06 out and up before Devlin could blink his eyes, and Devlin says he just took off running. He says McAniff shot at him five or six times, which agrees with the number of casings we found at the scene." Bill blew on his coffee and sipped at it. "Only nicked him once, on the outside of the upper right arm. Just like Becky Jorgensen. The McAniff specialty."

"Lucky for Mac."

"You know Devlin?" Jack nodded. "I think he was more than just lucky."

"How so?"

"I figure McAniff must have been getting tired. At any rate, he didn't pursue Devlin the way he did the others. He got back on the snow machine and drove down the road. And, as we

28

all know now, about twelve miles later he ran into Kate Shugak."

Not by a glint in the eye or a change of tone did Bill betray knowledge of Jack's history with Kate, or of Kate's previous employment on the Anchorage D.A. investigators' staff, but then he'd only been with them himself for eighteen months. While highly unlikely, it was possible the gossip had cooled off. Jack doubted it.

"Hers had been one of the homesteads Chopper Jim had warned on the way in," Bill said. "She took her shotgun out to the road, waited for him and bagged the bastard." He drank coffee and observed, "Too bad she didn't kill him."

"She wouldn't."

"Seems a pity. Would have saved us a lot of time and the taxpayers a lot of money."

"True."

"So." Bill began gathering the files into a pile. "What've we got here? One, two, three, four, five, six, six, seven, eight, nine, count 'em, nine murders in the first degree. Jesus. And one, two attempted murders."

"Those two attempts include the try at Mac Devlin?"

Bill looked up. "Of course. Why?"

Jack smiled, a small, wry smile but a smile nonetheless. "In the Park, shooting at Mac Devlin isn't quite the same thing as attempted murder."

"Then what is it?"

"I think it's more in the way of a team sport." Bill looked puzzled, and Jack said, "McAniff. Tell me about him."

Bill produced yet another manila file folder and opened it to the first page. "You know mass murderers virtually didn't exist until the sixties. Since then, there've been enough to begin building a profile."

"How fortunate for us."

"Yeah. Anyway, Roger McAniff fits the profile, so well it's scary. He's thirty-one, and M&Ms are usually in their twenties or thirties. He's five-six, which makes him a little shorter than average, and M&Ms usually are. He weighs in around one seventy-five, which makes him overweight, which also fits into the profile, but when you consider he's coming off an Alaskan bush winter, maybe that statistic doesn't mean very much in this case. He's got a mustache."

"Mass murderers got mustaches?" Jack said, smoothing down his own neatly trimmed mustache and beard.

"Most of them. Most of them are also usually white, usually male and usually likely to kill their victims in their victims' own homes."

"This guy is just typical as hell, isn't he?" Jack said, still stroking his beard.

"For a mass murderer," Bill agreed.

"When'd he move to Niniltna?"

"Last fall. He was working as a computer programmer for Alaska Petroleum."

"On the Slope or in town?"

"In town. There was a big rif—reduction in force—last September, and he got his pink slip then. About the same time his wife threw him out. According to the head of the Niniltna Tribal Council—" Bill squinted at a page. "Billy Monk?"

"Billy Mike."

Bill made a careful note. "Right, Billy Mike, according to him, McAniff showed up in Niniltna around Halloween."

"Enter the boogeyman."

"In person."

"From what we can tell without the autopsy reports, he's a pretty good shot."

"Expert." Jack raised his eyebrows. "Literally. In the army, '80 to '83."

"See any action?"

Bill shook his head. "He was stationed in Panama. Not much going on there then."

"Didn't re-up?"

"Nope. Transferred to Fort Richardson in '83, took his out here."

"Army have anything to say about him one way or the other?"

"No, pretty much standard evaluations all the way across the board. However." Bill flipped to another page. "You'll like this. When the troopers searched his cabin, they found a computer printout of the names, phone numbers and home addresses of Parks Department employees, and another of Department of Public Safety employees, including fish hawks and the State Troopers' own Alert Team. Nine of 'em." He looked up. "Including Jim Chopin.

ABOUT
KATE SHUGAK

KATE SHUGAK is a native Aleut working as a private investigator in Alaska. She's 5 foot tall, carries a scar that runs from ear to ear across her throat and owns a half-wolf, half-husky dog named Mutt. Resourceful, strong-willed, defiant, Kate is tougher than your average heroine – and she needs to be to survive the worst the Alaskan wilds can throw at her.

To discover more – and some tempting special offers – why not visit our website: www.headofzeus.com

MEET THE AUTHOR

DANA STABENOW was born in Anchorage, Alaska and raised on a 75-foot fishing tender. She knew there was a warmer, drier job out there somewhere and found it in writing. Her first book in the bestselling Kate Shugak series, *A Cold Day for Murder*, received an Edgar Award from the Mystery Writers of America.

Follow Dana at stabenow.com

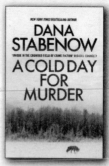

NEW YORK TIMES BESTSELLING AUTHOR

DANA STABENOW

'UNIQUE IN THE CROWDED FIELD OF CRIME FICTION' Michael Connelly

A COLD DAY FOR MURDER

NEW YORK TIMES BESTSELLING AUTHOR

DANA STABENOW

'ONE OF THE STRONGEST VOICES IN CRIME FICTION' Seattle Times

A FATAL THAW

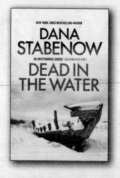

AN OUTSTANDING SERIES' Washington Post

DANA STABENOW

DEAD IN THE WATER

NEW YORK TIMES BESTSELLING AUTHOR

DANA STABENOW

'UNIQUE IN THE CROWDED FIELD OF CRIME FICTION' Michael Connelly

A COLD BLOODED BUSINESS

NEW YORK TIMES BESTSELLING AUTHOR

DANA STABENOW

'ONE OF THE STRONGEST VOICES IN CRIME FICTION' Seattle Times

PLAY WITH FIRE

NEW YORK TIMES BESTSELLING AUTHOR

DANA STABENOW

'AN OUTSTANDING SERIES' Washington Post

BLOOD WILL TELL

NEW YORK TIMES BESTSELLING AUTHOR

DANA STABENOW

'UNIQUE IN THE CROWDED FIELD OF CRIME FICTION' Michael Connelly

BREAKUP

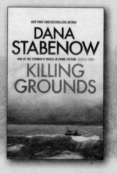

NEW YORK TIMES BESTSELLING AUTHOR

DANA STABENOW

'ONE OF THE STRONGEST VOICES IN CRIME FICTION' Seattle Times

KILLING GROUNDS

NEW YORK TIMES BESTSELLING AUTHOR

DANA STABENOW

'AN OUTSTANDING SERIES' Washington Post

HUNTER'S MOON

DANA STABENOW

'UNIQUE IN THE CROWDED FIELD OF CRIME FICTION' Michael Connelly

MIDNIGHT COME AGAIN

DANA STABENOW

'UNIQUE IN THE CROWDED FIELD OF CRIME FICTION' Michael Connelly

THE SINGING OF THE DEAD

DANA STABENOW

'UNIQUE IN THE CROWDED FIELD OF CRIME FICTION' Michael Connelly

A FINE AND BITTER SNOW

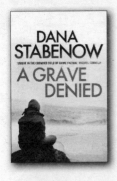

DANA STABENOW

A GRAVE DENIED

DANA STABENOW

A TAINT IN THE BLOOD

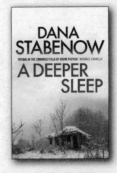

DANA STABENOW

A DEEPER SLEEP

DANA STABENOW

WHISPER TO THE BLOOD

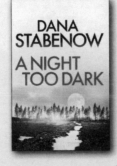

DANA STABENOW

A NIGHT TOO DARK

DANA STABENOW

THOUGH NOT DEAD

DANA STABENOW

RESTLESS IN THE GRAVE

DANA STABENOW

BAD BLOOD

DANA STABENOW

LESS THAN A TREASON

DANA STABENOW

NO FIXED LINE

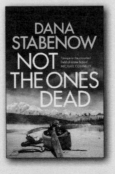

DANA STABENOW

NOT THE ONES DEAD